ICE AND A CURIOUS MAN

Also by Renée Angers

Wasted Land
Missouri
Catwalk
Blood
Breaking Rage
Small Dog

ICE AND A CURIOUS MAN

Renée Angers

Published by
Bladud Books

ACKNOWLEDGMENTS:

Shane Helnsley poetry excerpts
by John Dempsey © 2001/2002

THANKS TO:

Leon Unruh, Editor, Alaska.com
for all his kind help.

CHAPTER 1

'I might get the fingers to start turning flips
and the language will spill
like some 5 gallon box of wine'

Excerpt from 'Ugly People' by Shane Helnsley

It's not as if she had anything better to do for the next month of her life – just writing a bunch of redundant articles and reviews on the local music scene in St. Louis. It wasn't that she hated her job at 'Room', a small, alternative entertainment paper, but it really *had* become tedious. Her nights would typically be spent attending shows, which never left her any time to finish her current novel. Finish... that was funny. She had never gotten past jotting down a few notes long hand in a cheap pharmacy notebook. It was just an idea in its most embryonic stages. She knew, however, that if she had found the time, she would never get around to submitting it in anywhere, anyway. *'Too many anys,'* she concluded.

Then there was the perpetual hangover. A thick skulled feeling that she wasn't altogether certain was caused by the loud music every damn night, or the drinking she felt she needed to participate in to tolerate it. Just an occupational hazard, she supposed, while she would continue to pound them back.

Regardless, she had accepted this latest assignment and here she sat, in the back of a taxi cab headed for Lambert-St. Louis International Airport. She was so preoccupied with dreading the trip that she barely noticed when the car pulled up to the front entrance. She paid the unkempt and rather unsavory taxi driver and grabbed her laptop and bag off the seat. "Excuse me, Sir. What time is it?"

"Mmmeahey forhee fi."

"Pardon?" she asked, but the car squealed away before she had a chance to hear him repeat his answer. She wasn't even given the chance to close the car door properly. She reacted by shooting him the finger and hoping that he saw it in his rear view. "Asshole!" she mumbled under her breath.

She had forgotten her watch in her rush to get out of the apartment on time, but forgave herself for allowing her impending terror to steal her organizational skills away from her. She was positive that her loss of wits was only temporary and the result of a mild phobic anxiety toward flying. *Mild* – that was the understatement of the week. She was already two Dramamines into the game and her head felt like she was witnessing the world through a snug fitting sandwich bag.

Her flight was at five after nine in the AM and she had been warned to get to the airport at least one hour beforehand, preferably two. The largest of the clocks on the wall in the airport read eight fifty, meaning that the cabby's "Mmmeahey forhee fi," meant eight forty-five. She hurried at full gallop through the airport trying desperately to get a good hold of her luggage, but the bags kept slipping off her shoulder.

She reached the counter huffing wildly, trying to ask for directions while catching her breath. The woman behind the desk directed her to the proper terminal with a one-dimensional smile and the overwhelming stench of cheap hair spray.

Marren's hurried pace had her forgetting just how horrified she was of flying, and before she knew it she was on the plane and settling in.

She glanced around at all the safety blurbs, taking note of

what each said, but wanting to ignore them the way everyone else was. Everyone else seemed so calm. Too calm. *'You're all just too fucking calm,'* she thought.

She pulled a compact out of her bag and checked her reflection. She didn't look nearly as flustered as she felt. Her fire red hair was still neatly tucked away in its tidy ponytail. The minuscule amount of make-up she wore seemed in place and her flushed complexion from the rush only made her radiate a healthy looking glow.

The flight attendant passed by and Marren asked when she would be able to get a drink. "Not until we're in the air, Ma'am," she said. Marren smiled at her pleasantly, not much liking the answer but accepting it readily enough. Still, she was fairly certain that all the passengers in first class could enjoy a drink whenever they damn well pleased. Probably had a glass of champagne offered to them upon boarding. Spoiled upper class brats.

Her painfully polite smile fizzled off her face as the flight attendant moved on. Marren wished she had tripped the Barbie impersonator on her way by, but kept her thoughts silent. *'Ma'am? I can't believe she called me Ma'am. Hey lady, I look way younger than you do. And MY tits are REAL. Christ, why did I take this job?'*

She knew very well why she took this job. It was an opportunity to break into a larger market. One published novel didn't deliver nearly as much recognition as she had hoped and working for *'Room'* wasn't her idea of an exceptional stepping-stone in her writing career. She was still tightly wedged into a dollar more than minimum wage, and still a nobody.

At first, she was thrilled that a large national publication wanted to hire her. 'Literary Today' was no small potatoes – it was the big boy of its kind. The bad ass of literary magazines.

Gavin Preston, the Editor in Chief, called Marren himself, asking to meet with her. She agreed. How could she not? She wasn't crazy. Even if he had her mistaken for someone else, which she felt had to be the case, she jumped at the chance for a meeting.

She went to his big chic office and he quickly sat her down and then flung the proposition on her. She asked him if he was sure he had the right person and he assured her that he did; he then offered her the job again. This time it hit her like a pillowcase full of doorknobs and she wasn't even able to form words in response. She just sat there staring at him, her jaw too frozen in shock to even dangle stupidly. After several long moments, she began to stutter, "I . . . I . . .", but he interrupted her.

"I know this must come as a bit of a surprise." He smiled. "Why don't you take a couple of days and think on it. Get back to me when you've decided to accept."

She had met Preston a few years earlier when he wasn't such a bigwig. It was some kind of awards banquet and Marren was only there as a favor to a friend who had been nominated for something or other and begged her to be his escort. She really couldn't remember the specifics, nor did she care to. She didn't remember it as one of the more pleasant chunks of her life.

In any case, now Gavin was the head man at 'Literary Today'. He was still as friendly and personable as she remembered him to be. One might expect such an esteemed title to spawn an egomaniacal transformation of startling proportions, but Gavin was a gracious as ever.

As Preston suggested, she sat on his offer for a few days, then called to meet with him again. She went to his office for the second time and was treated like she was his best friend. She found the treatment odd, but didn't question it. The proposition, or "assignment" as he called it, sounded kind of adventurous . . . exciting even, but that quickly wore off when Gavin mentioned the subject matter she would be investigating and writing about.

She was to fly to Dillingham, Alaska, and get the full story on a reclusive poet named Shane Helnsley. She knew the name well. Shane Helnsley started at Oklahoma State University teaching English Literature and Poetry. Although his work refused to follow any of the rules he taught at the University, it was much sought after and he had a collection of his poetry published very quickly. He was rumored to have lost his mind and run off to Alaska with little else than the shirt on his back. This only made his work much more in demand. Unfortunately, over the years he very seldom released any new work to the public, prompting every interviewer and journalist in the country on their knees, begging his agent for some answers. They were usually just given some vague excuse or thrown a table scrap of old Helnsley work.

Helnsley had apparently agreed to an interview just recently, but only under his own very strict conditions. This is where the whole idea gave Marren an extreme case of the willies. His conditions were that the writer was to come alone, bringing nothing but their writing tools. There was to be no recording equipment of any kind. No tape recorders. No cameras of any sort. And . . . the writer was to be the one of his choosing: Marren Lang.

Why in the world would Helnsley choose her? She knew she had never met the man before. Not ever. She'd never even seen a picture of him. How had he heard of her? Gavin told her that he didn't ask and didn't know, " . . . but does that really matter? This is Helnsley we're talking about."

Marren chewed on the inside of her lip for a moment, all the rumors about Helnsley thick and all consuming in her thoughts, and then opted to just blurt out her concerns. "I've heard that he's . . . "

Gavin stopped her with an amused laugh and then proceeded to assure her that Helnsley was, in every sense of the word, a gentleman.

"Well, how do you know that?" Marren asked. "If you don't mind me asking."

"A colleague of mine has a friend that has met him several times," Preston said, reclining back in his cushy leather chair.

"Oh, how comforting," she said.

"His agent also assures me that he's a very well mannered man."

"Really? Well, I kind of find that hard to believe," Marren said. "All I have to go on are all those rumors I've heard and read."

"Most of them, Marren, are not true. He's a brilliant man. He's just very . . . secretive."

"Yeah. That was the mildest thing I heard."

"Don't tell me," Gavin started, holding his hand up. "You heard that he's a dirty old man. Completely mad and bordering on psychotic. He's John Merrick."

"Check. Check. And check," Marren smiled, ticking her finger off on an imaginary clipboard.

"No," Gavin said, looking altogether too sure of himself to know what he was talking about. "Don't worry. He's a bit . . . how shall I say . . . eccentric, but very bondable."

"Bondable?" Marren laughed. "Interesting choice of words."

"For an interesting man. Actually, Shane Helnsley is a fascinating man and I think you'll like him. Besides, this may be the one job that's going to push your career into high gear. Do you know how many writers would kill to be in your position right now?"

"I know. I know. It's just weird," she said waving her fingers around spookily. "I mean, why does he want *me?*"

"His agent says he respects your work," Gavin answered.

"But I write reviews on bands . . . "

"I think he meant your novel."

"What would Shane Helnsley read a smutty romance for?" Marren asked, finding that airing her question out loud only made the whole idea sound that much more ludicrous.

"Maybe he likes that kind of thing," Gavin suggested. "In any case, Marren, I really must know if you are going to accept this assignment. It is, after all, up to you, but I really don't think you should pass this opportunity up. I hate to make you feel rushed, but we need to make arrangements . . . you know, travel and what not. Helnsley's agent is pushing for this to happen now, before Helnsley changes his mind."

The flight attendant picked up her microphone, asking for everyone's attention, then began running down the safety instructions. It was, Marren supposed, the usual spiel. She wanted to listen, but her distracted mind only half heard what the attendant was saying.

She was surprised to find that she was able to get through the take off without digging her nails into the arm of the businessman sitting next to her. Actually, it really wasn't all that bad. Once they were in the air, she decided that it would probably be best to refrain from looking out the window until they were safely back on the ground. Just the thought of glancing out the window gave her a sticky feeling of vertigo. She went to close the window blind and got a glimpse of the sky outside. Her heart pounding hard in her chest, she took a closer look, only to see that it was beautiful, especially so above the clouds.

After an hour in the air, she finally had the drink she

wanted so desperately earlier and was feeling much more relaxed as a result. She hadn't eaten anything due to her apprehension toward flying, and that together with the couple of Dramamine she had swallowed, meant she was definitely feeling much more calm. Noticing that it was only ten AM, she looked down at her drink before partaking. She summed that it was seven AM in Alaska, and felt guilty for drinking so early . . . but she was sure no one was keeping tabs on her. It had to be happy hour somewhere in the world. Just the fact that she was being hurled through the air at a speed of 565 miles per hour in a hunk of metal that weighed in at 147,000 pounds . . . it just seemed unnatural. The wings weren't flapping. Nothing was flapping for that matter, and as far as she was concerned, this enormous thing she was sitting in just shouldn't be in the fucking air.

She opened her laptop to start taking a few notes on what she wanted to discuss with Helnsley (the psychotic freak), when the businessman seated next to her introduced himself. "Gary Crenshaw," he blurted out.

Marren looked up at him, seeing what she thought was an unthreatening smile on an even more unthreatening face. "Marren Lang," she responded.

"Nervous of flying?" he asked, peeking down at the glass she held clenched in her white knuckled hand.

Marren followed his eyes down to her scotch, neat. "It shows, huh? Uh . . . yeah, a little. Well, a lot, but I'm OK. Other things on my mind to be freaked out about."

"On your way to Anchorage?"

"Mmmm," she affirmed. "Overnight. I'm chartered out to some God-forsaken bush in the morning. Some place twenty miles outside Dillingham." She looked over at him, taking in the obviously expensive pin stripe and tailored suit. "You an accountant?"

"Investor," he corrected. "You?"

"Writer," she said, taking a sip from her drink.

"Oh, a writer. Very good. Novelist? Journalist?"

"A little of both, I guess you could say," she said.

"So what's in Dillingham?" Crenshaw asked.

"Some sour old pervert of a poet. I'm supposed to interview him. Shane Helnsley. You ever heard of him?" She knew it was absurd, but somewhere in the back of her mind she hoped he would say *'Yes. I've known him since we were boys. Good man. Very proper and trustworthy. Nope, no mental illness there,'* but he didn't.

"Helnsley . . . sounds familiar. But I'm not an expert on poetry."

"Join the club," Marren said.

"You don't sound very pleased," he observed.

"I'm not. I mean, this is a great opportunity for me. It'll probably improve my career prospects . . . It's just that . . . " She stopped herself and looked over at the stranger sitting next to her. "God, I'm a mess. I don't even know you and I'm telling you my life story. I'm sorry."

"No, no," he said. "You've got me interested now, and we've got . . ." he looked down at his very pricey Rolex. "Nothing but time and a bad movie. You were saying that this thing will be great for your career but . . ."

"See . . . he *chose me!*" Marren griped, her inability to understand the whole idea very obvious. "Helnsley has never given an interview to anyone before. Ever! Now he's finally agreed to give one but only under his own really strange and strict conditions."

"Sounds intriguing."

"Well, that's what I thought until I found out he actually picked me to do it. That was one of his conditions."

"There were other conditions?" Crenshaw asked.

"Yeah. No recording equipment. No cameras. And I'm to come alone. Me."

"Why you?"

"I don't know. He says he respects my work," Marren told him.

"You must be a very well known writer then?"

"Hardly," Marren laughed. "I write reviews on the local music scene in St. Louis. I've written one smutty romance that was published through a small press but it didn't do very well. I don't know Helnsley. Never met him in my entire life. I've read his work and it's wonderful. I can't figure out why on earth he would ask for me. Then, there's the little matter of him being a complete lunatic."

"This just keeps getting better," Crenshaw chuckled. "Tell me about this . . . lunatic."

"He's a recluse. He left his life and his teaching position at Oklahoma State to live like a savage in the middle of nowhere. The last frontier." She laughed nervously. "I've heard nothing but horror stories about him. People have actually referred to him as the 'missing link'. To be honest with you, Mr. Crenshaw . . . I'm absolutely terrified. I've never been so terrified in my life."

"You know what . . . I bet it will end up being really boring and then be over with before you know it."

"I'm there for a month," Marren muttered.

"A month? Wow. Is this Helnsley paying for your hotel?"

"I'm staying in his guesthouse," Marren said. "I'm told his home is too far out to commute every day."

"Guesthouse? Hmmm... he must have money," Crenshaw said, assuming a guesthouse meant that he had a large home.

"I guess," Marren agreed, finishing her drink. "Where are you off to?" she asked, feeling like she needed to change the subject for her own nerve's sake.

"Anchorage. Business. Nothing nearly as interesting as your situation."

They chatted about investments and financial portfolios. Interest rates and mutual funds. Capital gain this and stock market fluctuations that. Marren pretended to understand and to be interested, but quite frankly, she didn't and wasn't. Regardless, the conversation busied them for the next hour and a half, but then Marren's two Dramamine and three-drink breakfast demanded an urgent nap. She slept a numbed and drugged sleep for the next two and a half hours. Upon waking she read some of Helnsley's work, companioned with another dose of whiskey. Her stomach was beginning to feel an uncomfortable and empty rot from the lack of food and the alcohol, but it wasn't anything that couldn't be numbed with another drink.

As she read, she came to see just how amazing Helnsley's writing was. His work was absolutely incredible. She found herself wanting to cry one moment and laugh out loud and hysterically the next. The tears would be of pity or heartbreak. The laugh – of amusement, or total revulsion. The work followed no grammatical rules whatsoever and it appeared that he just let it all flow without any predefined or patterned obstacles, and then let it lie there gasping for breath like a wounded animal. He made her feel a strange ache and an even stranger itching frustration. It was as if his printed word itself *was* frustration and that frustration infected anyone who came into contact with it. Shane Helnsley's work was a disease. A very contagious and debilitating disease.

The flight finally ended, landing at Anchorage International Airport at two forty-five PM, Alaska time (five forty-five, hers). She dragged herself and her bags out to the front exit of the airport, her legs stiff yet rubbery from the lack of space in the economy section. She had heard tell of people suffering from blood clotting after longs flights and imagined herself having a stroke right there on Helnsley's front step. There she would lay, convulsing and flopping around like a big, slimy, foolish fish, surrounded by Helnsley's servants. "Who is she?" one would mumble in a Ukrainian accent.

"She's the writer," another would whisper.

And then Helnsley himself would appear, pushing his way through the crowd rudely and as forcefully as his hobbling age would allow. He would gaze down at her, babbling insanities through brown spike-like teeth, spittle dribbling out the corner of his mouth. His bald, liver spotted head shining in the white Alaskan sun causing near snow blindness. Beads of sweat clinging to his wrinkled and quivering upper lip. She imagined him kneeling down beside her and begin howling and masturbating. The entire scenario repulsed her, but also caused her to start laughing.

She hailed a cab and put the ridiculous images out of her mind. Her legs were fine and with the amount of alcohol she consumed on the flight, she was certain her blood was running quite thin. She willed old babbling Helnsley out of her mind. She refused to have him take up the bulk of her thoughts until she absolutely had to allow him to be there. Instead, she focused on a hot shower, a cold beer, a meal and a good night's sleep.

She called Gavin once she arrived at her hotel to let him know that she had arrived. Then she called to confirm her charter for the next morning out to Helnsley's home. It was to leave at nine, so she planned on being at the airport by eight. This "two hour prior to" bullshit was for those anal retentive travelers that like to sit around and guard their luggage against those evil flower toting Krishnas. Nine times out of ten there were never any complications with tickets, and more often than not any problems with flights were delays. Why did passengers need to arrive two hours prior to boarding if boarding wasn't to take place until a delayed sixteen and a half hours after the scheduled time? Her flight was a charter, so she wasn't about to start worrying about all these moronic rules and regulations. One hour was going to have to be enough.

After showering and helping herself to that much anticipated beer from the mini-fridge, she ordered room service and then selected a movie from the pay-per-view in her room. 'Bill and Ted's Excellent Adventure' and 'Trainspotting' were the only choices. The latter was the obvious choice, for obvious reasons. It was the perfect prescription for a mind requiring intelligent distraction. The brilliance of the film would do nicely, so she allowed the first five minutes to pass by without turning it off, which allowed the hotel's billing mechanism to kick in. It may be the last time she ever saw a good film. It may be the last time she ever saw anything for that matter, considering that she was about to spend the next month with that psychopathic relic of a man. She quickly brushed the thought out of her mind reminding herself of Preston's description of Helnsley as "bondable". Wasn't that the word he had used? Well, if you're going to be a mad axe killer, you may as well be a bondable one.

With a full stomach and another beer to her name, she found it impossible to stay awake any longer. She clicked off the television three quarters of the way through the movie and crawled under the blankets. She was out cold before her head hit the pillow. Seven-thirty PM.

The wake up call came in at seven AM, taking ten rings to successfully bring her into consciousness. She didn't think she needed the call, being a habitual early riser, but she was proven wrong. She hung up the phone and rubbed at her face groggily. This must be what they mean when they say 'jet lag'. She felt tired in a very thick sort of way, like she had gotten *too* much sleep but needed more.

She called room service and ordered herself the standard Continental breakfast. She showered while she waited, looking forward to it, but once it came she was only able to push half the croissant down. It would seem that her meeting with Helnsley had come complete with its own set of appetite dissolving butterflies.

Arriving at the airport at twenty to nine, she was again running. At the main counter she asked where she would find her reserved charter going to Dillingham.

"The name?" the young man asked.

"Marren Lang," she said.

"Could you spell that, please," he asked.

Marren took a deep breath to keep her patience. "M-A-R-R-E-N-L-A-N-G"

"Lang. Lang . . . Oh, here it is. It's reserved under the name Heln . . . Helnsley. A Mr. Shane Helnsley."

"That's right," she said, starting to tap her foot as the minutes ticked by.

"Well, this charter isn't going to Dillingham, Miss Lang. It's going a bit further north than that."

"Yeah, well, whatever. Can you just tell me where I have to be?"

The clerk gave her directions and she was off running again. She found the terminal easily enough and jogged over to two men standing by the exit, talking.

She excused herself and showed her reservation to them, asking them if they could help her out. The more casually dressed of the two smiled at her. "Ah, you're the writer I'm takin' out to Shane's place."

Marren nodded, panting and feeling relieved that her hunt for the plane had ended. "Yes," she panted, fighting to catch her breath.

"I'm the pilot," he said. "Follow me."

The pilot said his so-longs to the man he had been speaking with, then led Marren out through the gates. Outside stood waiting the small Cessna Skylane that would deliver her out to her dreaded assignment. Its wingspan stretched for what looked like thirty feet, maybe more. For some reason she felt safer with the idea of being hurled through the air in a hunk of metal that was a tad bit more compact than the monster she had sat in yesterday. Still, she swore, it just wasn't natural, even if the physics behind this plane were a little more believable.

"Nice day to fly," he said. "I'm Ed by the way. Ed Lawry."

"Marren Lang," she returned. "I'm the only one on this flight?"

"Yup. Shane wanted it that way."

"Do you know him?" Marren asked.

"Shane? Sure I know him," Ed replied.

Ed helped her climb in then shut the door behind her. He walked around to the other side and climbed in himself. Marren's eyes darted all over the instrument panel, and then over to Ed. He smiled as if he were the happiest man on the planet. "Sure is a nice day."

He started the engine and the propeller began to whirl. Marren felt that familiar poke of terror's pointy finger in her stomach. She realized that she had forgotten to take a Dramamine and immediately began frantically hunting through her bag for them.

"Forget something?" Ed asked.

"Dramamine."

"Don't worry about it, Miss Lang. I've got a good stash of air sickness bags."

"Great," Marren mumbled sarcastically.

She found the bottle, fumbled to get one out and stuffed it in her mouth quickly. Ed smiled. "We'll be there before that thing even starts working."

"It's more of a mental thing," she informed. "Knowing it's in me calms me down." The plane started to move, turning slowly to make its way toward the runway. "Can I talk to you while you fly, or do you need to concentrate?" she asked.

"You can talk, I can talk, we can both talk at the same time. Hell, I can sing show tunes for ya if ya like."

Marren laughed at Ed's unpredictable response, then her face became serious. "What's he like?"

"Shane? He's a great guy," Ed said.

"Great like what?" she prodded.

"Well, he's real friendly. He's kinda private, but not in an anti social kinda way. He's friendly. Real friendly."

"So he's not nuts?" she pushed.

"Shane? No . . ." Ed answered. "Well, maybe just a little. Don't tell him I said that."

"How old is he?" she asked.

Ed frowned slightly with thought. "Ya know, I'm not too sure. Now that ya mention it, I don't know. I never asked him." He peered over at her quickly, giving her a wink. "Rest assured, he's old enough."

Marren found herself turning her nose up at Ed's answer. It came across as perverse and she decided right then to give it up. Just go out to Dillingham, or wherever it was she was going, meet the weird old coot, do the best job she could do and reap the rewards later. Both Gavin and Ed said pretty much the same thing about Helnsley. She felt like she should be reassured about her safety. She hadn't been hired to write the memoirs of a serial killer. *'Don't be so silly,'* she told herself. All the same, she was out in the middle of nowhere to interview some eccentric and possibly dirty minded old crust of a poet.

It *was* a nice day. Clear. The Cessna flew low enough for Marren to appreciate the spectacular scenery that was Alaska.

She had had no idea it was so striking. It was so immensely breathtaking that she felt stupid for never allowing herself into a plane before. She had been born, bred, and rarely ventured very far outside of Missouri.

Ed made small talk with her, asking her what it was like to be a famous writer. She looked over at him and then broke out laughing. "Why don't ya ask Helnsley that?"

"I did," Ed said. "All's he said was that he needed a drink. So now, I'm askin' you."

"Well, I'm not famous," she said.

"Shane said you're good. He said you've got something. He told me that out of the few rough diamonds he's seen, you shone the brightest of the lot."

"He said that? How corny! Who is this guy?"

"Yup, that's what he said," Ed confirmed. "He always has a way of putting things. And as far as he goes, he told me he was just a lump of coal that didn't want the pressure."

CHAPTER 2

She didn't know how long they had been in the air; maybe only about forty-five minutes or so. It could have been over an hour for all she knew. Ed told her he was going to circle the clearing below, and come up from it on the other side. "Easier for me to take off again," he said.

"We're here?" she asked.

"We're here."

He circled around the clearing, just like he said he would, and then began his landing maneuvers. Marren thought her anxiety would escalate again as the plane descended, but found that her discomfort with meeting Helnsley far surpassed her petty phobia. She gathered her wits and took in a few secretive deep breaths hoping she would find the strength to meet him without trembling and perspiring too profusely.

The Cessna's landing was a little bumpy, but all in all, virtually painless. Once they were on the ground and came to a full stop, Marren looked over at Ed. "Am I supposed to hike to his house from here?" she asked.

"Depends on what ya think a hike is," Ed smiled. "That's Shane's house right there," he finished, pointing across the clearing.

Marren peered out the windshield to see a tiny little cabin. "*That's* his house?"

"Sure is."

Marren's deep breath wasn't as concealed as her previous few, and held more of a discontented manner about it. She gathered her things, unbuckled herself and opened the door. "Thank you, Ed. It really was a pleasure meeting you."

"Pleasure was all mine," Ed said. "I'd pop in and say hello myself, but I'm runnin' a little late. Tell Shane I said Hi. I'll be out for a visit soon."

Marren smiled and closed the door, then turned and began walking through the overgrowth toward the sorry looking little hovel. It wasn't necessarily in bad shape – actually it looked quite solid and well kept – but it was so small. "My washroom is bigger than this place," she muttered under her breath as she tromped through the tall, dried, yellowed grass.

Once at the stoop, she turned to see Ed lift off into the deep blue sky. Her heart sank as the reality of her situation set in. She felt alone. Very wary, vulnerable and alone. She climbed the three steps, one of which was loose, and moved up to the door. There was a note on it:

'Marren Lang - Around back.'

She sighed heavily and turned around, stepping off the porch again. She made her way around the side of the house, struggling with her bags. Coming around the back corner she heard a striking sound and then a moment later she saw a young man chopping wood in the far end of the yard. She approached him, trying to get his attention by calling out to him . . .

"Excuse me . . ."

He appeared to be in his late twenties. He had shoulder length dirty blond hair and was shirtless. "Um . . . EXCUSE ME? HELLO?" she tried again. "I'M LOOKING FOR SHANE HELNSLEY."

"Marren Lang," he said, whacking his ax into the tree stump he had been chopping wood on. He walked over to her, wiping his hands on the thighs of his loose fitting green

26

work pants. They hung so low on his hips that Marren thought for a second that if he rubbed his hands on his thighs one more time, they would drop right off of him. He did and they didn't.

He stuck his hand out to her and she took it. "Hi," she said. "Is Mr. Helnsley around?"

"Yeah," the young man said in a low and gruff, but friendly voice. "You're lookin' at him."

Marren's eyes grew wide as she stared at the young man in front of her. "You are . . ."

"Shane," he said.

"No you're not," she smiled. "Oh, I get it . . . you're his son. Is your father around? I'm looking for Shane Helnsley . . . the poet."

He looked down and laughed a little, then peered back up at her. "My father died twelve years ago, and he wasn't no poet. I'm Shane Helnsley. I'm the so-called poet."

Marren just stared at him, her expression painfully stunned. She didn't say anything at all, simply stared. She couldn't believe it. The man standing before her was young and, quite honestly, criminally attractive. "But you're . . ."

Just then, her bag slid off her shoulder and she struggled to grab it. Shane reached over and snatched it before it hit the ground, taking it from her. "Lemmee help you out here," he said, taking her other bag as well. "You were expectin' someone a bit older I reckon. A lot of people think that. I played a little trick on them, but you'll find out all about that later," he said. "C'mon. I'll show ya around."

He walked away toward the house, leaving Marren to stare at him from behind, dumbfounded. He turned around a moment later, noticing that she wasn't following. "Ya comin', or do I have to carry you in too?"

That said, Marren woke up, took in a cleansing breath and

followed him into the house through a back door. The house smelled like wood, fire, cigarette smoke, and strong coffee. It was dark inside, but not dismal by any means. It looked comfortable. Cozy.

"This, obviously, is the kitchen," he said, walking through it, his heavy boots clomping loudly against the wooden floorboards. He motioned for her to follow him into the next room. "This is the living room," he said, passing through it to another doorway. "Bedroom," he said, nodding inside. "And the privy," he smiled, pointing to what she guessed was the bathroom.

She peeked inside the bedroom to see nothing but a bed with a small table next to it, a raw wood dresser and a wood burning stove in the corner. She then glanced into the washroom to see a large old tub, a toilet and an old fashioned sink with the two spouts. He passed by her on his way back toward the kitchen and turned his walk backwards to face her. "Ya want a cup of coffee or somethin'?" he asked.

"Um, no thanks," she replied. She looked around the living room but only did so to keep her eyes off of him, not because he was so immensely easy to look at, but because he was the last thing she had ever expected to see.

"How about a real drink?" he asked.

"Pardon?"

"Ya look like you could use it. I can smell it in your writing too. Ya like to take a belt once in a while, don't ya?"

"A real drink would be fine. Thanks," she said, trying not to smile too much. What did he mean, 'he could smell it in her writing'? Was it that obvious? It wasn't like she was an alcoholic or anything, was it?

Shane disappeared into the kitchen and she took the opportunity to try and absorb the shock she still felt after meeting him. She glanced around the living room again – this time, actually taking everything in. There was a stone fireplace . . . nice. Over on the far wall, under the window, was a large oak desk. On it sat a computer, and a telephone with its cord wrapped around itself – obviously not hooked up. There were stacks of books and papers all over the top covering any possible work area. Evidently the desk was not in current use either.

A small sofa rested directly in front of the fireplace by about ten feet. It wasn't long enough to be a regular sized couch, but it was larger than a love seat. Over in the opposite corner from the desk, sat a comfortable looking armchair, and a large shelving unit that contained a surplus of books and yet more stacks of paper. Next to the chair sat an off balance reading lamp. Other than that, there was only an enormous rug that everything was sitting on.

There wasn't much in the room, but it held exactly what it needed. Any more would have been too much. She liked it. She felt it was charming. No overkill. No confusion, except for the confused mess on the desk, but even that looked to be comfortably at home.

A moment later Shane returned with two glasses and an ancient and very decorative looking bottle of something unlabeled and amber under his arm. He offered her one of the old fashioned glasses and then filled it for her. "This is Ed's pride and joy – I mean, aside from his plane," he said, letting his eyes drift from the glass up to hers. "Ed. He flew you in."

"Ed. Yes. Interesting man," Marren said, lifting the glass under her nose. The aroma was a little like whiskey, but she couldn't be sure. "Whiskey?"

"The best," Shane said. He poured himself a glass, then corked the bottle back up. "Ya don't say much, do ya?"

"I'm sorry. I'm just really, really surprised," she admitted. "I heard that you were . . . well . . . not at all what you are."

"Yeah," he mused. "I planned it that way," he added, tipping the glass but keeping his eyes on her.

"You planned . . . what? I don't get it," she said, taking a small sip out of her own glass as a test. The liquid's warmth didn't start in her throat like all other whiskeys did, but it started right on the tip of her tongue, and as she swallowed, its warmth spread throughout her insides like a gigantic security blanket with a fantastic sense of humor.

"C'mon outside. I guess I got some explainin' to do," he said.

She noticed that his southern accent was still quite pronounced. Well, why wouldn't it be? He hadn't been out here that long.

Her mind was swimming with all of this. Just the anxiousness she had felt toward the trip, and the uncertainty of meeting Helnsley, had her adrenaline pumping a steady flow since yesterday morning. With her body now filled with it, she was beginning to feel its numbing affects. It was almost as if she was removed from everything going on around her. Distant and ghost-like. It was all quite exhausting.

The man in front of her said something, but she was somewhere else. She didn't notice until he smiled at her. "Anyone home?"

"Pardon?"

"Are you OK? Ya seem kind of far away."

"I'm fine," she answered, shaking the bats out of her head. "I'm sorry, just tired I guess."

"Well, c'mon outside and sit down."

Again, she found herself following him and once out on the front porch she sat down on the step, but made sure to keep her distance. "OK, start explaining," she said. "Just don't shock me anymore than I already am. I'm too spent."

"Well, what do ya already know about me? Just so I don't become more tiresome to ya."

"Um . . . I know that you were an English professor at Oklahoma State for about two years . . . wait . . . how can that be? You don't look more than twenty-five, twenty-six."

"Thirty-three," he corrected.

"Really? You don't look it," she came back.

"This place. It's kind to more than the spirit," he told her.

"You're thirty-three?" she asked, needing to confirm what she thought she heard.

"And counting."

She took a moment to accept this, looking into his face and noticing his soft brown eyes. There was the faint evidence of aging, but the very few almost invisible lines around those warm brown eyes were only the shadow of the character they would become. "Still," she said, "You're very young to hold such a high position."

"They called me a genius when I was fourteen, and the fun never stopped after that," he said. He sipped out of his glass, and then seemed to speak only to himself. "They. Who the fuck are *they* anyway and what do *they* know?"

"I also know that from 1992 to 1994, your works were published in various magazines and books, and critically acclaimed as well."

"*They* again," he mumbled.

"Then, in 1994, your book was published. '*Ugly People*'. But soon after that, you picked up and left to come here. That's all I know for sure. Other than that, all I've heard and read are rumors."

"I started them," he said. "A list of character flaws as long as my right arm and physical deformities as long as the other."

"Why?" she asked, finding it unfathomable that anyone would do such a thing.

"This is off the record, right?" he asked.

"If you want it to be."

"Yeah. Please."

"OK. Off the record," she agreed. "Why?"

"I got a glimpse of success and I ain't never seen anything so ugly, but by the time I figured that out, it was too late. My success was something that has been following me around all my life and when I wasn't lookin', it just fell right into my lap. I didn't ask for it. I didn't even work for it. Just all of a sudden, there it was in my lap. A big sloppy mess of ugliness. Everybody wantin' a piece of me. So . . . I put a stop to it. I paid a lot of people to deny they knew me and counted on a few others to be real creative in describing my person to anyone that came askin' any questions.

"It wasn't easy, but before too long I was this toothless, deformed, ninety-year-old man that had lost every last one of his marbles and took a certain pleasure in pleasin' himself every chance he got . . . if ya catch my meanin'. My agent has done a great job keepin' the whole thing goin' for me. I owe him a lot. He's a good friend," he finished.

"You're still famous, you know. Maybe even more so," Marren informed.

"Yeah," Shane agreed, sounding disappointed.

"So, you did all this just because you didn't want success?" she asked.

"It's the way people treat ya," Shane said. "If you aren't a big important person with piles of money, you're nobody. No one cares. I've seen people with no one – not a fuckin' soul carin' about them – and it's ugly. If you have a name and a few bucks, everybody wants to be your best pal."

He looked over at Marren. "Why would I want to be best pals with someone that has no sense of empathy, no sense of decency? People that would just as soon run over you in their car and leave ya there to die? The greed, selfishness, and expectations of these creatures didn't make sense to me. I just wanted out."

His words struck her hard. It seemed to her that his animosity toward society ran a little deeper than he was letting on. "So it's your disgust with society that brought you out here?" she asked.

"Yeah . . . that's a part of it," he answered.

"Do you hate everybody?"

"No, not hate," Shane said. "Dislike."

"Do you dislike me?" she asked, smiling and feeling amused with his over the top disapproval of the human race.

He peered over at her with a look on his face that was stone. "No, I don't." It was a look that bore right through her and she needed to look away. Then he added, "So, all my best pals and biggest fans wanna know what's goin' on, huh?"

"Yes, they do," she said. "So what do I tell them? I mean, you're not that twisted old masturbating maniac wearin' Kleenex boxes on your feet." The whiskey was catching her off guard and making her feel rather free to poke fun at him.

Shane laughed and gazed over at her. For a fleeting instant, she thought he looked familiar, but it quickly passed. It was the softness in his eyes. "Sure I am," he said.

"You are?"

"I am."

She stared at him, unable to stop smiling but feeling that she didn't understand him. "I'm sorry," she said. "I'm just more bewildered than I've ever been in my life."

"You ain't bewildered. Ya just ain't drunk yet," he said.

Marren decided, although it seemed like she didn't even make the decision herself, that she was beginning to like this man. "Is there anything else I should know?" she asked.

"Do ya know how to fish?" he asked.

"Fish?" she repeated. "No, actually I don't."

"Well, you should know how to fish. Everyone should know how to fish. I'll teach ya."

With her stare fixed on him, she found his simplicity terribly attractive and willed herself to not look away. "Why did you ask for me to write your story?"

"I read your book. I like your style," he said.

"It's a mindless romance," she laughed.

"No it isn't," he stated strongly. "The way I read it, you took the idea of romance, or what western civilization sees as romance, and you shit all over it. You brought romance back to its most primitive beginnings. It's thick. You chose raw passion over all that perfumey crap. You found the limbo between romance and eroticism and I'm sure you pissed a lot of people off with that find. You've got the guts of it."

She felt flattered by his words, but disagreed with him. "I think you read a little too much into it."

"I don't think I did. I taught this stuff and I think I have a pretty good eye for it. I think you have it."

"OK," she said, raising her eyebrows and still disagreeing with him.

"Your writing – is it from your fantasies or is it from experience?" he asked.

Marren looked over at him unable to decide whether his question was too forward or just the inquiry of a very respected English Prof. She pondered that for a minute and allowed herself to answer him truthfully; after all, he was being honest with her. "Fantasy. There is no such thing as perfect love."

He emptied his glass and smiled. "Fantasy is good," he grinned. "You're a very passionate woman. Your writing will do just fine. This is gonna work out just fine."

He lit a cigarette and offered it to her, then lit another

for himself. He snapped his zippo shut and stood up. "Let's walk."

They strolled out across the clearing together and their conversation waned. It was a little while before Shane finally spoke. "I don't want ya goin' out by yourself. Least for a while. It's pretty easy to lose your way around here and ya never know when you're gonna run into a wolf or a bear or somethin'."

"Bear?" Marren repeated.

"Yeah. There's tons of them around here. Black, Brown . . . I've even seen a Cinnamon Black hangin' around. She's somethin'."

"Oh great," Marren mumbled, sarcastically.

"Bears are cool," Shane said. "Respect them and they'll respect you. Whatever you do, don't get between a mother and her cubs. Actually, don't go anywhere near a cub . . . ever."

"I'll make a mental note of that," she chuckled.

They crossed through a patch of tightly grouped trees. Marren could hear the sound of water moving and slapping against rocks, becoming louder with each step. Just before they emerged from the trees Shane put his arm out in front of her to stop her. "Be real still," he whispered as he crouched down and urged her to do the same. "Speak of the devil. We got a female Black out there gettin' her lunch."

"Where?" Marren whispered in return, feeling oddly safe with him.

"Right over there, in the stream," he said quietly, shimmying up close to her and pointing.

Marren's eyes followed the direction his finger was aimed to see a shiny, pitch black bear staring down into the water. She pounced on a fish and then lumbered up on to the bank with her catch. She dropped it to the ground and it flopped around violently, but she plopped one huge paw down on it, probably killing it. She then settled down to eat it. Marren recalled her thoughts about suffering a stroke from the flight, on old man Helnsley's mansion porch, flopping around the way the bear's lunch did. She smiled, pulled her eyes off of the bear and planted them on Shane's profile. There was no stroke, and there was no old man. With the trip, the fear, Ed's home-made whiskey and this insanely attractive man crouched next to her, she was, for the moment, very pleased to be exactly where she was. She returned her gaze to the bear and they watched intently for several long minutes. "God," Marren breathed. "She's beautiful."

Shane looked over at her, seeing her smiling. "Ya like that?" he asked.

"Definitely," she nodded, unable to take her eyes off of the sight.

"Good," he said, quietly.

They watched for a little while longer, then snuck back through the trees the way they had come. Once they were back out in the open, Shane began to talk again. He told her stories about his first few run-ins with bears when he had first relocated up here. He made her laugh. He made her feel on edge, waiting for his next word with excited anticipation. She was enjoying his company so much, she had actually forgotten that she had been hired to come here and interview him. She had forgotten who he was, and who he was supposed to be. Shane Helnsley – poet extraordinaire.

It was getting close to five PM and Marren sat on the back steps while Shane moved the wood he had chopped that morning under a protective wooden canopy next to the house. She watched him quietly, taking note of how much more relaxed she was. That ghost-like feeling of not being a part of what was happening around her was no longer a surrounding entity. Her body had worked off the adrenaline overdose and her mind was not so noisy.

Load after load, Shane carried armfuls of wood across the yard. She had offered her assistance, but he said that if he accepted her help and decided that he liked it, he was liable to want to become lazy. He told her that she would be helping him enough with her writing and left it at that.

"So, how did you find this place? This house?" she asked.

"I built it," he said.

"You built it? You're kidding, right?" she smiled.

"No. I bought the land and built it," he said. Marren was still looking as though she didn't believe him. "I came up here not knowin' what the hell I was gonna do. All I knew was that I needed some quiet and to get away from everyone. I needed to work for what I needed.

"I met Ed Lawry and he took me around lookin' for the land I needed. I liked this spot so I worked through some red tape and bought it. Got myself some wood and built my house."

"Got some wood?" she repeated. "You make it sound like an afternoon project. Were you a carpenter before or something?"

"No. Just needed a house. How hard could it be?"

Marren thought about what Gavin had said to her just before she accepted the assignment. He said that she would be staying in Helnsley's guesthouse for the month. All there was around here was his house and a shed where he had put his ax away earlier. There wasn't even a garage for his truck.

It had been on her mind since she arrived, but she was hoping that through the course of the day he would have said something about it. He hadn't, and even though it was still looking like high noon, her body was telling her that evening was lowering itself down on them quickly. She had heard tell of the long Alaskan days, and this time of year the sun rose at around four in the morning and set close to eleven at night.

She had entertained the notion of bringing one of those sleep masks with her, but assumed that after a few days she would become accustomed to the bright nights. No matter, still heavy on her mind was where the hell was his guesthouse?

"Um . . . Shane? Gavin Preston said I would be staying in your guesthouse."

"Yeah. That's right," he said, a shrewd smile creeping up on his face.

"OK," she said. "So where is it?"

"Right there," he answered, nodding his head at his house.

"*This* is your guesthouse? I thought this was *your* house."

"It is. It's my house, and this month I have a guest."

She had been smiling, but the smile seemed to have frozen on her face. It lost its flavor and left her looking like a heavily outlined comic strip character. He began tossing older and drier pieces of wood through the back door and into the house as she stared at him. He was well aware that his little joke about the sleeping arrangements weren't tickling her at all.

"No worries. You can have the bedroom and I'm takin' the couch out in the living room," he finally clarified.

Now her smile died altogether. Although his clarification sounded a little more acceptable, it also sounded very unfair to this host that had been so far nothing but courteous to her. "It's OK. I'll take the couch," she said.

"Actually, I can't allow that," he said. "Besides, it'll be a good change for my back. Ya gettin' hungry?"

He stepped over her on the steps and vanished inside the house. Marren remained sitting wondering just how many more surprises were in store. All Shane had done since she had been here was amuse and charm her. She had just found out that there was no guesthouse but it wasn't upsetting her. She was miles and miles away from anything that even remotely resembled a motel, and although she knew she should be furious, she giggled quietly finding her entire predicament quite entertaining.

Shane re-emerged from the house, popping his head out and asking her if she wanted to join him for a beer. She didn't even have to think about it before she said she would love to. A moment later, he came out and handed her one. It wasn't a brand she knew of, and whatever it was, it wasn't American.

He sat down next to her, a little closer than she had allowed herself earlier, and looked over at her. "Hope ya like fish. We ain't got any fried chicken and waffle joints anywhere nearby."

"Fish is fine," she chuckled. "You caught it yourself, I assume?"

He nodded. "I pretty much catch and grow everything I eat," he said. "It's one of the ways to escape the indolence that has plagued our culture."

Marren raised her eyebrows, as if his statement had collided with what she had expected him to say, and it definitely left a small dent. She had nothing to say in return, and settled to just move the conversation on if only to keep from laughing at him. "I guess you cook, too?"

"I ain't no galloping gourmet, but I make do."

"Poet. Fisherman. Carpenter. Philosopher. Cook. What else do you do?" she asked.

"Wouldn't you like to know?" he smiled, getting up and making his way over to the canopy.

He grabbed five pieces of wood and chucked them over to the fire pit. He arranged them with his foot, then walked off in the direction of the shed. He grabbed some kindling and came back out, placing them down as well. He felt the chest pocket of his untucked and open flannel shirt, only to find that it was empty. He lifted from his crouch and smiled at Marren as he passed by and into the house. He returned back outside moments later with a box of matches in his hand and resumed his stance next to the fire pit. He lit the kindling in several areas, then bent down low to blow on the struggling flames.

She was only human. She couldn't help but watch as he took in deep breaths and expelled them slowly into the fire, helping it grow and burn with a hot intensity. Her imagination lifted to a level she did not wish it to go, but its disposition seemed to have a mind of its own. She too, took in a deep breath but hers was not to fan a flame; hers was to cleanse herself of the less than honorable thoughts that had entered into her mind uninvited.

Within a few minutes, Shane had the fire up and going satisfactorily. He got up and sat back down with her as he waited for it to get hot enough to cook on. "That was fast," she said.

"Ya get good at shit ya need to survive with," he told her. "I'm sorry about the guesthouse thing."

"I'll get over it. I'm pretty resilient," she reassured.

"Good," he said. "I'd rather gnaw my own leg off than send ya home with any painful emotional scars."

"Do you ever say anything that isn't amusing?" she asked.

"One of the few things I don't get to do a whole lot of out here is talk to people, so when I get the chance, I do my best to entertain."

He cooked some Northern pike and whitefish in a cast iron skillet that sat on a flat rock in the center of the flames, and baked a couple of potatoes. They then retreated into the house to eat, as the sun was taking on an eerie white chill.

After dinner, Shane started two more fires. One in the fireplace and one in the wood burning stove in the bedroom.

He had taken Marren's bags and placed them behind the bedroom door. He returned back out to the living room and sat down on the sofa, looking over at Marren as she sat before the fire he had built. She gazed into it, watching its hot fingers snap and flicker. "It's almost unbearably quiet here."

"Does that bother you?"

"It's strange."

Shane nodded. "I'm used to it."

"I can hear myself breathing and that kind of freaks me out," she finally said.

He was quiet for a moment, watching Marren listen to her own life. "What else do ya hear?" he asked.

"My damn heartbeat," she answered.

Shane laughed, then offered her a challenge. "Listen real close for a minute and tell me what else you can hear. I can pick up five things."

"Other than my breathing and my heartbeat, I hope."

He laughed again. "Yes, other than your breathing and your heartbeat."

Marren tilted her head as if it would activate some kind of invisible radar for her. "Crickets," she said.

"That's one," Shane said.

Marren listened again, needing to strain, but she didn't get anything. "No."

"The fire," Shane said.

"Oh well, of course. Yes I can hear that, obviously."

"But ya didn't notice it."

"You're right, I didn't."

"What else can ya hear?"

She listened hard, squinting her eyes, but got nothing. She shook her head.

"The wind," Shane pointed out. "Don't ya hear it in the trees or moving past the house?"

His question motivated her to listen even harder and after a few seconds she could hear what he was talking about. "OK, yes. What else?"

"The water running from the stream to the lake . . . and a raccoon going through the garbage out by the shed."

"Really? Right now?"

"Yup. He will likely be at it for a while, and make a few trips back tonight," he told her.

"Well, won't he leave a mess?"

"No," he said. "Way I look at it, I've already made the mess. Why should his be any worse?"

"Well, because *you'll* be the one cleaning it up, not him."

"Hell, that's OK," he said, taking a hit from his beer. "Only difference between his mess and mine is that mine is organized. All neatly tucked away in bags and cans ready to be hauled away and dumped somewhere where we can all ignore it and pretend like it didn't happen. One of the human race's dirty little secrets."

"You sound like you have something against your own garbage," Marren chortled.

"I guess I do. Everything we make is taken from what the earth has generously given us. We manipulate it, melt it, mold it and destroy it until we have the end product we just can't live without, right? Lord save us if we had to live without it. Then when we've used it or become bored with it, we give it back to the earth as trash that can't be broken back down into its original state. It's perverse."

"Are you an activist?" she asked.

"No. I'm a coward," he replied.

"A coward? That's kind of harsh. Why would you say that?"

"Because I chose to run away from everything that I don't want to look at. All the perversions."

"Garbage being one of them?" she smiled.

42

"Garbage being one of them," he smiled back. "But the truth is, I can't get away from it. If it isn't in front of me, it's already in here," he said, tapping on his temple.

"Garbage," Marren said.

"Everything," he said. "As for garbage, we can recycle it until we're blue in the face. We can correct injustice with compassion and stomp out greed by being a charitable soul. We're all just a bunch of hypocrites. What we as a race have already done to ourselves is just foreplay. We haven't even started to fuck ourselves yet."

"You definitely are Shane Helnsley," she said.

"Every God damn day."

A hush fell between them, filling the room with a thick soupy tension. "Mr. Helnsley, you're a curious man."

Just then, one of the logs in the fireplace popped loudly, spooking Marren. A moist air pocket in the wood then released a high-pitched whistle that escaped the living red fibers in a stream of steam. Outside there was a muffled thud and then the sound of angry animal chatter. The pop in the fireplace was one thing, and something Marren could explain, but the sounds outside were alien to her. They bit down on her nerve endings and tugged at them, feeding her already teetering state of uneasiness.

"What the hell is that?" she asked.

"Coons," Shane answered, smiling at her. "Sounds like someone is defendin' his supper."

"Defending it from what?" she begged.

"Probably another 'coon."

"Raccoons don't make any noise, do they?"

"Sure they do. They speak up when it's necessary. They can get pretty ornery, too."

Marren's hand rose to her chest in an attempt to calm her pounding heart. Shane chuckled a little. "Ya need another drink?" he asked.

"No. I guess I'm a little jet lagged. I'm already half-way in the bag." It was true. Her speech hadn't yet been affected, or not so much that it was noticeable, but she really was feeling drunk and one more drink would surely finish her off.

"Ed's Juice packs a punch too. It nips at ya all day. If you ain't used to it, it'll get the better of ya," he said.

"Does it get the better of you?" she asked.

Shane smiled. He could say a million things right now, all of which would be very clever, but also very inappropriate. "Not the way I would like it to," he said.

"What does that mean?"

"I'm still a coward," he muttered.

"God, you really aren't what I expected. I can't get over it," she said, staring at him.

"Are ya disappointed?" Shane asked.

"Are you kidding?" she spat. "Have you looked in the mirror lately?"

"What does *that* mean?" he asked, repeating her own words.

"Touché, right?"

"Yeah . . . that's right. Answer the question."

"It . . . I . . . Well, I just, I wasn't expecting a hot lookin' guy, that's all."

"Ya like the way I look?"

Marren just realized what she had vocalized and wondered just what exactly was in that damn whiskey. She had just backed herself into a corner and Shane was right there in front of her, waiting for an answer. "I just said that out loud, didn't I?" she smiled. "I didn't mean it . . . I didn't mean to."

"You didn't? So ya *don't* think so?" he asked.

"No . . . I mean yes . . . I mean . . . Ah, fuck it. Yes, I think so."

Shane's smile hadn't dwindled, but grew. He nodded

and stood up to make his way toward the kitchen. The sun had sunk quite a bit lower now causing the new darkness of the kitchen to swallow him as he entered. A moment later, Marren heard the back door open and shut. She wondered what he was doing but dismissed it knowing that she probably wouldn't understand it anyway.

He really was a curious man. What was going on in that mind of his was something she really would have enjoyed digging out of him and giving to all the die-hards out there that wanted to know, but he seemed to want the lies kept alive. The lies. All the rumors and stories were nothing but hired tales designed to deter the public from asking of him more than he was willing to give. He was a genius that appeared to be haunted by his own thoughts and actions. His problem was that he was too willing to accept the reality that he could do nothing about what he called 'the perversions'.

Desires and good intentions aside, as one man he really couldn't mend the damage he felt mankind caused, or ease the ugliness of society. Who could? He felt that being a man himself automatically dubbed him a representative of the race that disgusted him and that . . . that he had to run from.

If their discussions of this day were any indication of how they would go for the rest of the month, she could very possibly return with one hell of a story. The truth. What if she brought back the truth? Gavin Preston would shit himself and her success would be assured.

She laid her head down on her arms as the heat from the fire relaxed every muscle in her body, or was it that damn whiskey doing it? Regardless, her eyelids were so heavy she couldn't keep them open any longer.

Shane came back from checking to see if there were any casualties from the raccoon feud. He returned to the living room to find that Marren was out cold; not the casualty he was expecting. He crouched down next to her and just watched her for a moment. He slid his arms under her back and her knees and picked her up. As he carried her to the bedroom she woke slightly and wrapped her arms around his neck, burying her face in his hair. "Oh God, you smell good too," she mumbled in a sleepy voice, too exhausted to realize what she was saying.

He placed her down on the bed gently and took her boots off. He covered her with two thick blankets, checked the stove one last time, and then left the room closing the door over behind him.

Sitting back on the sofa, he grabbed her half finished beer off the floor and took a sip out of it. Feeling hot in front of the fire, he took his shirt off, and as it brushed his face he noticed something: the scent of her had taken up temporary residence in the flannel collar. He brought it up to his face and breathed it in for a moment before placing it over the back of the couch. Sitting back, he lit a cigarette, inhaling deeply and then letting it escape in a long blue stream. He didn't notice, but he had pressed his tongue up to the roof of his mouth and the muscles in his jaw worked tensely. He didn't want to say what was fighting to get out of him but found it slip past his lips with the smoke anyway . . .

"How long's it gonna take for me to make you love me?"

CHAPTER 3

The aroma of embers in the wood burning stove and bacon from the kitchen woke her. The sun was beaming into the room right at the base of the bed and it took a moment to realize where she was. She was in Nowhere, Alaska, in Shane Helnsley's house . . . in Shane Helnsley's bed. Panic rose up inside of her. She had gotten herself quite drunk the night before and wasn't sure what she had said or done. She held her breath and peeked under the blankets to find that she was still fully clothed. She let her breath out with the force of relief behind it. The door was closed over and she sat up, rubbing at her face.

Her head hammered as though it was going to burst open and splatter its contents all over the room. She had one of the nastiest cases of gut rot she'd ever had the pleasure of. Crawling out of bed slowly, she made her way directly toward her bag, pulling out a bottle of aspirin she had packed. Finding her way to the washroom next door, she washed her face and took three aspirins, drinking them down directly from the tap. She remained in the washroom for a few moments waiting to see if she was going to throw up. Her ears had heated up and her face tingled, the room became fuzzy and unstable in her vision, and her legs felt extremely shaky. All the warning signs were there. Splashing cold water on her face halted the sensation. She still felt unpleasantly nauseous, but knew any contents of her stomach would remain there and under her control.

Upon exiting the washroom and entering the kitchen, the smell of bacon caused another slight poke at her stomach, but it passed as she sat down. Shane was obviously just out of the shower. His hair was still wet and all he wore were his pants. He was standing over the stove making breakfast when he saw Marren come in.

"Mornin'," he greeted. "Did ya sleep alright?"

"I have no idea," she mumbled, still wondering what she had said and done the night before.

"Coffee?" he asked.

"Yes, please," she replied, sounding as if she was in desperate need of it and would most certainly succumb to a very sorry demise without it.

Shane poured her a cup and placed it in front of her, eyeing her. "Ya hurtin'?"

"Very."

Shane immediately grabbed the bottle they had started the day before and poured her a shot. He turned and offered it to her. "Oh, Jesus Christ, no."

He crouched down next to her and smiled. "If there's one thing I *am* good at, it's this," he said. He took her hand and wrapped her fingers around the glass, forcing her to take it. "Plug your nose and down the hatch. Ya may puke, but chances are pretty good ya won't and you'll feel a lot better if ya just do it."

Marren took the glass as she peered into his eyes. She sighed, plugged her nose and downed it. Shane searched her expression. "Ya need to be sick?"

"I don't think so," she said, searching herself. "Damn, that bacon smells good all of a sudden," she added.

"Success," Shane smiled, standing from his concerned crouch.

Marren stared at him as he continued to see to the food. "Shane, may I ask you a question?"

"Ain't that what journalists do?" he came back.

"This one is just for me," she said.

"Go ahead," he replied, stirring the scrambled eggs.

"Did I say anything last night that may have . . . that was . . . unsuitable?"

"Well, that depends on what ya think unsuitable is," he answered.

"You know . . . did I . . . flirt with you?"

"Well, you said I was hot lookin' and that I smelled good. Is that flirtin'?"

"Oh God," Marren said, covering her face. "I'm sorry. That stuff," she said, giving the shot glass a push, " . . . is intense."

"Ed calls it truth serum," Shane told her. "I just call it Juice."

"I'm so embarrassed. I hope this doesn't change your feelings on having me work for you. I was real tired and . . ."

"Hey," he said, stopping her. "It doesn't change a thing. Ya wanna know what ya did? You made me feel real good and that ain't nothin' for you to feel bad about."

"I did?" she asked.

"Yeah. Ya did," he answered, putting her breakfast down in front of her. "Now, eat. It'll kick the shit out of the rest of that hangover."

"I hope so," she said, still feeling the headache jabbing at her.

"It will. And then you'll be ready to start all over again."

"Oh no!" she said. "I've got a job to do."

"Job shmob," Shane said. "The job'll get done a lot better if you're havin' a good time. Nobody wants a job that sucks." She peered up at him and then started laughing. "Plus," he added, "I like gettin' the compliments."

After breakfast, she showered and dressed for the cool weather with a thick pair of socks, a bulky sweater and a pair of long johns under her faded blue jeans. She found Shane out on the front porch repairing the loose board she almost broke her neck tripping on when she arrived. With her note pad and a pen readied, she joined him, sitting on the top step. The muscles in his arms flexed under his tanned skin as he planed the board that had swollen so that it no longer fit in its spot.

"Aren't you cold in just a T-shirt?"

He glanced up at her. "No. Thick skin."

She flipped to the first page of her notebook. "OK, So, how do we start this?" she asked. "Can I ask you when you write? What motivates you?"

"You could," he said, without looking up. "I'm always writing."

"What do you mean?"

"Up here," he said, tapping on his temple as he had the night before. That, she remembered. She remembered the little things with large gaps between them. "Just never get it down on paper," he finished.

"A lot of your pieces have this sick kind of emotion in it. An odd kind of romance. The public believes you write about a real woman. Rumors are that she was a woman from your past. Is there a woman? Is she real?"

"As real as if she were sittin' right in front of me," Shane said, looking up at her.

She didn't have a right to, but she felt a small squeeze of jealousy take her. What lucky woman could win the heart of a man like this? She must be absolutely gorgeous. Marren could practically picture her. Naturally blond, no doubt. Curvy and perfect beyond belief. She felt ashamed and embarrassed by her slight twinge of envy. This was the man she was basically working for. This was Shane Helnsley. Get a grip.

"You still love her." It wasn't a question; she was stating a fact.

"I never didn't," he said.

"Does she know? You write as if she didn't. As if she had . . . died," she said, feeling certain that any woman that had his love surely wouldn't let it slip away.

"She's very much alive. She's more alive than I could ever be, and no, she doesn't know," he answered, choosing a piece of sandpaper from his toolbox. He folded it and began sanding the area he had planed.

"She doesn't? I bet you she would want to."

"Maybe," Shane agreed. "And maybe someday I'll tell her, but I like feelin' like this and if she knew, the poetry of the romance would be over and the pain would start."

"What pain?" she asked, not understanding him.

"Maybe she wouldn't love me back," he said. He had stopped his work and was gazing directly into her eyes.

She wasn't writing any of this down. It was his, or so she felt. No one should be able to look that deeply into a man's heart. No one except the woman he was talking about. And thank goodness he changed the subject . . . "How's that hangover?"

"Gone," she smiled. "I left it in the bottom of that shot glass. I guess we should get started then."

"As good a time as any," he agreed.

She watched him work a moment longer, then yanked herself back into reality and poised her pen on the paper's surface. "I'm not going to write down what you just told me. None of my business really. How would you like this to start?"

"We just keep the gag goin'," he said. "See, my protective shell has been wearin' a bit thin lately and I need to put a few more coats on it."

She had a feeling this was going to be the direction he wanted to take and didn't question him. He looked up at her expectantly, hoping she would agree to his request, but her initial silence worried him. Her expression was uncertain for a few seconds, then she looked down at her paper. "OK, let's start paintin', old man."

Shane smiled.

She pondered for a moment, then scribbled down her opening to his story . . .

> *With his right hand smoothing back his sparse and matted gray hair, he clutched and fiddled with himself through his pants with his other.*
> *Shane Helnsely, a man of literary brilliance, sits in a rickety old chair on the porch of his shanty, slobbering out vulgarities through a mad and toothless grin. The three unsightly and cauliflowered cysts on his forehead are difficult to ignore, but he assures me that they have stopped growing and only weep occasionally.*
> **'Literary Today':** *Mr. Helnsley, why the silence for so long?*

Marren read her rough draft of an opening to him, needing his approval. He laughed. "Cauliflowered? Nice," he said.

She asked him the first question she had already jotted down and looked over at him, awaiting his response . . .

> **'Shane Helnsley':** *There's no silence here.*
> **'LT':** *Allow me to rephrase that question, Sir. Why have you decided to not release any further works since 'Ugly People', nor granted anyone an interview until now?*
> **'SH':** *Allow me to latch my gums on to that sugary rack of yers and I'll promise ta answer that kes-chun fer ya.*

The words popped out of Shane's mouth quickly and phonetically, making it obvious that he had been living with this disguise for quite some time. It was second nature for him to summon the old man up. Marren had stopped writing after she heard the word "rack", and she peered up at him. She didn't lift her head at all, only shifted her eyes toward him. A smile slowly crept onto her face. Shane noticed the silence and looked up at her from his work. Seeing her grin prompted his own until they both burst out laughing. It was strange. Almost as if they had always known each other and had become the best of friends.

"That'll go over well," Marren said, composing herself.

Shane pounded another nail into the now flush fitting board while she finished writing his previous answer down.

'LT': *Mr. Helnsley, people say you are insane. How do you feel about that?*
'SH': *I feel like I got the world by the balls. The tighter I squeeze, the wider their eyes open. If I were to spit in my hand and rub nice and soft, the world would be coming on my doorstep . . . then they'd fall asleep. Tell 'em I think they're insane.*
'LT': *You seem very preoccupied with sex, Sir. If I may be so bold, may I ask how a man of your age keeps his energy?*
'SH': *It's a loaded gun, Missy. Ya don't keep your gun oiled and in use, it's gonna seize up on ya. Ya gotta pull that thing out as often as ya can and shoot it. Ya gotta keep it workin'. Ya gotta keep pullin' on that trigger.*
'LT': *Your mannerisms seem to contradict the gentler emotion in your poetry. Why is that?*
'SH': *Where'd ya hear that? That ain't true. You rest assured, Missy. I may write the pretty words about love and pain and romantic shit like that, but you can be sure I got my dick in my other hand while I'm doin' it.*

Marren laughed again, then looked up at Shane and pulled in a deep breath. "This is really weird," she said. "Tiring."

"That's why I knew it would take a while," Shane told her. "I didn't think I'd be able to keep the act up too long. Truth be known, I hate this guy and it's exhausting to think like him."

"He's kind of funny. I mean, in a repugnant kind of way."

"And you only just met him. I been livin' with this asshole for a couple of years now and he's drainin' me."

His explanation came across as sounding lunatic at best. The revolting old man had been invented by Shane. Created. Imagined. Yet his choice of words made it seem like he was as real as the two of them were. She floated around in his idea for a moment, trying to understand, and concluding that he must be right. Just sitting there listening to him had exhausted her. She had had enough hangovers in her life to know that the sensation she was experiencing wasn't that . . . it was more cerebral. Had the old man been real, she knew that she would not last more than a few days here. It was as Shane had said. His mannerisms were draining. Even though Shane hadn't actually acted them out, but only spoke his words, it didn't make the sensation of depletion any less.

Shane suggested that they put it down for a while. They could have some lunch and a drink, restocking their energies for their next run-in with the character. She agreed and found his suggestion to be very attractive, not because she was in dire need of lunch (well, maybe the drink), but because she found herself missing him. The real Shane. She could only assume that he felt the same way. He must be missing his own wits.

"You know what this makes me think of?" she asked.

"What?"

"*The Exorcist.* When they leave the room after their first try," she mused.

"Yeah," Shane laughed. "Christ, and we gotta go back in there later."

As Shane finished up with his repairs to the step, Marren retreated back in the house to put her notebook away. She crouched down next to her belongings and went to shove the notepad inside a folder, but stopped. She peered down at it and then flipped it open to the few pages of chicken scratch she had just completed with him. The interview was nothing like she had hoped it would be the night before. He had wanted to "keep the gag going" as he put it. It was such a shame. What the world would do to know the real story and to meet the real Shane? The actual Shane. What that story could be and do for her compared to the bullshit that was staring back at her from the page was staggering. It would probably make her a million.

Quickly, she grabbed a fresh notebook and her pen and began to write as fast as she could . . .

'This interviewer has a truth to share that you may find shocking.

'We have all been tricked and made fool of. The hideous and perverse old man that was believed to be Shane Helnsley is nothing more than an invented character, created by Helnsley himself, to protect himself from the prying eyes of the world.

'The handsome thirty-three year old man resides approximately twenty miles north of Dillingham, Alaska, in a house he built himself. A sanctuary . . .'

She heard Shane enter the house and she quickly crammed her new set of notes down into the bottom of her bag. Just as she covered it over with some of her clothing, he rapped lightly on the frame of the bedroom door. His eyes met with hers, then they drifted down to her hands and their squirrel like movements as she hid the book. "Lookin' for somethin'?" he smiled.

"Um, yeah . . . my box of floppy discs. Found 'em," she smiled, holding them up. An unwelcome feeling came over her, flushing her face and feeling hot behind her skin. Just below the surface of the slight jolt she received, there was a queasiness that was laced with thick and unadulterated guilt. She placed the box on the case of her laptop and then looked back up at him. "I wanna get started putting it in my computer later tonight."

Shane nodded. "Ya want a drink?"

"Sure. Why not?" she said.

"Exactly," he said. "Why not?"

He made BLT's with the left over bacon from breakfast. The leaf lettuce and tomatoes were from his garden in the back and were sweet and fresh. The tomatoes were this beautiful pinkish color and had just enough tang to obliterate the need for any mayo or dressing whatsoever.

The last thread of her hangover frayed and snapped with her comfortably full stomach. Shane stacked the dishes in the sink, not allowing Marren to help do them. They could wait. He felt like walking.

They headed out the way they had the day before, only today there were no bears to be seen. Marren was still on her guard, though. She glanced around at the snowcapped mountains and glaciers in the distance, and into the forest that seemed to surround them. She knew they were roaming around out there somewhere and hoped to God that they weren't going to cross their path. She tried to occupy her mind with something else.

"When are you going to teach me how to fish?"

"Whenever ya want. Maybe tomorrow. Hope ya don't mind gettin' up at four in the mornin'."

"Four? Jesus! Why so early?"

"That's when they're active," he said. "I never got into the specifics of why, but that's when the catchin' is best."

"Fuckin' fish," she said.

Shane glanced over at her as they walked along the rocky bank of the stream. He smiled at her comment. "You got a great character," he said.

Marren crouched down and picked up a perfectly round and smooth stone. "Is that a compliment?"

"It is," he said.

"Well, thanks. I mean for thinking so."

"What . . . don't ya think you deserve compliments?" he asked.

"I dunno," she answered. "They just make me feel all sticky and uncomfortable."

"Well, I owed ya one," he said.

They strolled slowly along the edge of the seemingly endless and widening stream and Shane told her of the Native American lore. He pointed out a Golden Eagle and showed her the evidence of Otters by the bank. She took mental notes of everything he told her and everything he struck her as being, as well as trying to remember his words of the previous day. She would have to jot everything down later. It was far greater than anything she had expected. All the tales and bits of articulation that spewed out of him were going to snag the big bucks for her and she was tasting it.

Problem was, as much as she didn't want to, she liked him. She really liked him. Yes, he was eye candy, that was a given, but did he have to be so intelligent and personable? Did he have to be such wonderful company? Did he have to make her feel all woozy? This guy was special. But really, who the hell was he? After the month was up and she flew back to St. Louis, she'd never see him again. Why should she care if he was found out? So what if he gained the recognition Marren herself sought after? This was dropped in her lap, just as his success had been. She would be a fool to pass it up. Surely he would understand that. After writing this piece everything would come easy for her and all she had to do was rat him out. Point her finger at him as he cowers in the shadows of his lies. It wouldn't kill him. It wouldn't even hurt him . . . would it?

"Shane . . ." she started, breaking the silence of nature's orchestra. "Please forgive me, but I'm having a really hard time understanding why you feel so strongly about keeping up this charade."

"You'd have to be in here to understand," he said, jabbing himself in the chest with his thumb. "I don't expect you to understand, Marren. How could you? I had to take the chance that you'd be a friend. I'm seein' that you are and I'm hopin' I'm right. Your writing is capable of adding the one thing to my disguise that it's been missing – passion. It's kinda' like poetry. If there's no passion, what's the point?"

His answer to her question was like a shovel to the back of the head. "A friend," he had said. Ouch. Why did he have to say that? For that matter, how could one goddamn word pack such a furious wallop?

He could see that his words had troubled her. He was hoping that they would at least make some kind of connection with her, but now he was wondering if he had said too much. Perhaps he was slathering it on a bit thickly, but hers seemed to be a tougher hide than he had previously thought. He looked over at her and could remember with great clarity the first time he ever saw her and what she did to him . . .

CHAPTER 4

He knew her. He knew that face, and a maddening rush of panic overcame him for a moment. The panic would have been there regardless of whether he knew her or not, but he wouldn't have lost himself in that face if he hadn't known her. He spoke out loud, but didn't hear himself . . .

"Jesus, Marren. What have you gotten yourself into?"

He pulled his sport coat off – damn thing, he hated having to wear crap like this. It made him feel so blended and adult, but the one time he dressed the way he felt most comfortable, the Dean at the University told him that he looked like a student. Said that he would earn much more respect from his pupils if he dressed a little more presentably. "Not to mention the staff," the Dean added. "Now, it's really up to you, Shane, but let's just say that it's code around here." He may as well have just come straight out with it: dress like us or you're dismissed.

In any case, he folded 'the damn' sportcoat up quickly and placed it under her head as he simultaneously and very clumsily dialed 911 on his cell phone. Marren coughed, and blood sputtered out of her mouth as the operator responded.

"911."

"I got a hit and run here. I've got a woman down. She's hurt."

The voice on the other end asked him where he was and a sickening realization came to him. He didn't know where the hell he was. He was only in St. Louis for that fucking convention he wanted nothing to do with. He never expected to be wrapped up in this kind of situation. He didn't know his way around this city and was only going on the directions scribbled down by a friend.

He knew he was on Washington Avenue, but that was all. "Shit, I . . . I dunno," he stuttered. "Hang on," he said as he left Marren's side and jogged up to the nearest intersection about a half block down. "21st," he panted. "Washington and 21st North. About a half block down . . . on Washington."

He jogged back, his breathing now heavy, making it difficult to answer the operator's questions about what he had witnessed and Marren's condition.

"She opened her car door and out of nowhere a blue Lincoln Continental just rammed into 'er. Hit her and ripped her car door clean off. Look . . . she's down and she doesn't look too good. She's bleedin' a lot."

He knelt by her again. His coat under her head was now dyed a deep maroon and a small puddle of her blood was forming on the pavement. "Jesus," he said. "She's bad. Can you people please hurry?"

"They've been dispatched, Sir. Just calm down and stay on the line, OK?"

He put his head down to her chest but heard nothing. He placed his fingertips on her neck but felt nothing. "Ah fuck," he breathed. He dropped the phone and began doing CPR on her. He gently but quickly placed his hand under her neck and opened her airway, then pinched her nostrils shut, placing his lips against hers. He filled her lungs and then let go of her nose, watching her chest. No response. He repeated the steps, tasting her blood in his mouth. Then again, then again.

On his fifth try, she coughed and brought up a lot of blood. Shane tilted her head slightly so she wouldn't choke on it, then wiped it off her face on his white T-shirt. "It's OK. I gotcha. I gotcha," he said.

She opened her eyes and looked up at him. "What's happening?" she asked.

"Just be real still, Marren," he said.

"Who are you?"

"My name's Shane Helnsley. I'm a friend," he told her. "Don't talk. Just relax, OK?"

"Shane. That's a nice name," she said, a lazy smile surfacing.

"Thanks," Shane said, smiling back, trying to keep her with him. "Help is comin'."

"I don't know you, but will you stay with me?" she begged quietly.

"Yeah. I'll stay with you. You bet."

He could hear the sirens approaching and within' moments the ambulance pulled up. The paramedics quickly pulled out the gear they would need and dropped down to her side. "She's already been out once," Shane said. "But I got 'er back. She's bringin' up a lot of blood."

They placed a collar around her neck and then lifted her onto a stretcher. They worked on her at a wild pace as Shane picked up his coat. It was saturated, ruined, but he dropped it over his arm anyway.

The police had arrived, but Shane had already locked up his rental car and hopped in the back of the ambulance with Marren. The medic told him that they would want to talk to him and Shane said that they could talk to him at the hospital. "Just fuckin' drive."

The medic worked on her a little more, monitoring her vital signs. She looked up into the medic's face. "Where's Shane?" she mumbled.

He looked over at Shane. "I think she's askin' for you," he said. "He's right here, Ma'am."

Shane moved a little closer to her. "I'm here," he said.

She looked relieved. "Figures I'd meet the man . . . the man of my fuckin' dreams when . . ." she swallowed, "I'm dyin'." The pronunciation of her words was sluggish and sounding almost as though she was inebriated.

"You ain't dyin'," Shane said. "Just got a bump on the head. Goose egg."

Marren smiled groggily and stared at him for a moment, taking in as much as she could. "Liar."

As wrong as the idea was, as inconceivably vulgar as he found it, he had the strongest urge to kiss her right there and then. "I don't lie," he said. "It ain't my nature."

"My god, you're a good lookin' man," she gushed. "Wish I . . . I wish I . . ." She closed her eyes and slipped under again.

"You her boyfriend?" the medic asked, sliding the oxygen mask back on her face.

"Uh . . . no," Shane replied. "I saw the accident. I called it in."

"Well, I'm glad she likes ya. Looks like you're the last thing she's ever gonna see."

Shane glared over at the medic, finding his lack of compassion and his bedside manner completely obscene. Not only did this man's total disregard for the human life in front of him disgust Shane, it caused something inside of him to snap. A darkness that had been quietly hiding in his deepest soul bloated up inside him and changed everything. It made him really see what was going on in this life – a sight he had always forced himself to ignore. "It's good to know we're all in such good hands," he mumbled, but the medic didn't appear to get it.

"So, ya don't know her?"

"No, I know her," Shane said. "Her name is Marren Lang. She's a writer. A damn good one."

* * * *

62

The police reprimanded him for leaving the scene before talking to them and he merely took in a deep breath as if they were boring him. They asked him a shitload of questions and must have repeated her name for clarification a dozen times. "How do you know her?" they asked. He had answered this question at least ten times now and the officer was taking notes. Could he not read his own fucking writing? "Did you see the make of the car?" He did. Lincoln Continental. Light blue. Old. Beaten up. A lot of rust. "Did you get a look at the driver?" No. Not really. It happened too fast. It was a man, though. Caucasian. Dark hair. "Did you happen to get the license number?" Only half. The first half. 101, but he couldn't get the last three letters. "*Show me State,*" he muttered. "They should advertise this kind of shit for tourism."

That night he lay in bed, thinking. His flight back to Oklahoma was in the morning and he had a class at one that same afternoon. Would they miss him for a day? He didn't have to be back. It certainly wasn't unheard of that a class be canceled. Still, why did he feel the need to stay? Why was she on his mind? He forgave himself. He had, after all, witnessed a violent hit and run. It was savage and stuck in his mind with a repulsion that had him needing a drink. How could anyone do that? The vision of the hit was only a layer, however. A shell for what was clinging to him even thicker. The woman.

He had recognized her right away. It was Marren Lang, the novelist. He had crouched down next to her and ten feet away from where her car door landed in the street. The Lincoln had torn out of an empty parking lot across the street at an enraged speed, swerved right and raced right at her. It was as if the driver was actually aiming for her. The strike sounded like a large melon hitting the ground – a cracking kind of thud. The car door flew and then landed, hitting the road with an excruciating metallic crash. Metal sliding across pavement.

Her body was flung like a mop doll, six feet up and over by eight or more. She lay on her back, twisted at the waist but not in an unnatural way. He rushed over to her and as he crouched by her, she tried to get up. "I'm OK," she said, sounding quite normal. Every fiber of her wanted to get up, but she was broken and a sleepiness hit her like a two by four.

Her head had been split open, although Shane couldn't tell how seriously. He put his coat under her head as the blood dripped off the ends of her hair. He had called 911 and did everything he knew how to do. All he could do then was wait.

It had been three days since the crime and she was still implanted deeply in his mind. He felt horrible for thinking it, but it kept popping into his head – how beautiful she was and how he would have much rather touched her under different circumstances. In the photo on the back of her novel she was attractive to him, but in person, and even in her condition, she was stunning. She had a simple purity about her that he wanted to sink into.

Over the course of the next few months, he had made several anonymous phone calls to the hospital to check up on her progress. At first they didn't think she would make it. She had undergone two surgeries to release the pressure on her brain, and although her body was healing, it wasn't certain that her mind would.

He was able to get his hands on the *Post-Dispatch* – the St. Louis newspaper – with a little help from the internet, and read up on how the police were doing with their investigation.

It wasn't long after the hospital told him that she had come to and was doing well that he read in the paper that they found the driver of the Lincoln. Apparently it was her ex-boyfriend. It was a clear-cut case of an abusive relationship. She had a restraining order against him, but his stalking only became worse from there. He was not shy about why he did it either. He had been quoted as saying he wanted her to die. *"She'd go out to bars every night saying it was part of her f---ing job. I know what she was doing. She was f---ing all those rock and roll guys . . . I know. Whores like her have to be punished."*

He had been locked up in jail waiting for his court date, and then was convicted of attempted murder and several traffic violations including driving on a suspended license. He was sentenced to 120 months with possibility of parole in 64. Shane would have preferred to read that the son of a bitch was sentenced to be beaten to death, but, hey . . . no such luck, right? Not in this country. He himself would have been the first to volunteer for the task and completed it with as much pride as he could possibly muster.

During those months he had also found out that her family were notified but they never so much as sent her a card. What the fuck was wrong with people? The thought made him feel physically ill. She had been clinging to life in ICU for months and no one gave a shit about her. He could have gone. He could have taken some time here and there and flown down to visit in on her. Bring her flowers . . . you know, give her what she needed. A friend. He never did, although the temptation was nearly killing him. An itch he couldn't reach. He wondered if he had been working too hard and if that could be the reason he was thinking the way he was. It was almost as if he had become obsessed with her, and that possibility scared him.

She had been released from the hospital and was apparently almost one hundred percent. The nurse who had come

to recognize Shane's voice told him that they had been calling her 'the miracle' around the hospital. The only thing that
she was having trouble with were bits of her memory – more
specifically, her memories of the accident. The blow to her
head also caused her left eye to have just a very faint laziness
to it, but it didn't affect her vision at all.

He wanted to call so badly. Forget it.

He poured himself a shot of whiskey that just happened
to half fill a highball glass. He rummaged through the stacks
of term papers on the desk in the corner of his apartment. He
really should sit down and correct the damn things. Instead,
he pulled Marren's novel out from between them and a pile of
Post-Dispatch papers that he no longer had a need for.

He and his whiskey and her novel found their way over to
the sofa and he sat down staring at the front cover. He knew
all too well that she had had no control over what that cover
would be, and the subject matter left a bad taste in his mouth.
The artwork was typical and although it came across as not
bad in that sense, it was so typical it was second rate. A big
burly looking fellow with his shirt open displaying overly-
bulbous pectoral muscles that looked like he could probably
crush bricks into a fine powder between them. In his arms he
held a woman that Shane guessed was supposed to be gorgeous. She had massive breasts and her cleavage was spilling out the front of her dress. She, too, probably had super
human powers and could twist beer caps off between those
ungodly things.

He wondered how the art director that over-saw this trav-
esty even got his or her job. How could that art director sleep
at night knowing that what they scrawled their approving
John Smith on day after day was complete garbage. Appalling.
He took a sip from his glass and turned the book around to
look at her picture. She really was a beautiful woman. Long

fire red hair. Large almond shaped honey brown eyes and a charming dimple on her right cheek next to her well-defined lips. Her uncomplicated beauty had his mind reeling. "Fuck off," he mumbled to himself, turning the book over again, not wanting the feeling.

He opened the book and read her opening, finding it a piece of art on its own . . .

'Kiss me behind the church.
This could only be what Captain
Delicious would demand . . .'

Captain Delicious was the name she had given to the dreaded feeling of regret, which the reader would learn about later in the novel. Although it was a romance story, it had grit and guts. It was more a story exploring the intricacies of human emotion verses the lower animal passions and how obsessive love is given birth to somewhere in between. It spelled out how regret could transform into resentment. That inevitable need for the human heart to find something or someone to blame for what it lacks.

He really should correct those papers. He wondered what she was doing right now. Now that she was out of the hospital, what was she doing? Did she remember him? Did she remember his name or his face? If he were to surface in her life, would she reject him? The nurse said she was having trouble recalling that night at all, and even where she had been prior to the accident. Was it coincidence that after that God-awful banquet they would be out on the same street, miles away from the hall? What was she doing out there?

The hall was full of snobby publisher types, writers, journalists . . . you name it. He couldn't imagine why he had accepted the invitation to celebrate the birthday of some old fart that couldn't write poetry to save his life. There was some kind of award ceremony as well. A real potpourri of festivities.

He sat at a table with a colleague of his and they swilled whiskey together. He looked up at the door just as she walked in. She wore black dress slacks that curved around her hips softly. The black sequin-studded halter-top she wore caught the light and twinkled across the room. Her red hair cascaded over her bare shoulders, and sat beautifully over her gently generous assets.

Shane's friend followed his stare across the room. "That's Marren Lang. Journalist for some little Gen X grunge rag."

Shane knew who she was. He'd read her book and loved it. "Who's that she's with?" he asked.

"Mmmm, some big shot at the *Post-Dispatch*. Local paper. Movie review guy I think."

"They together?"

"I don't think so. Just friends as far as I know."

Shane nodded and continued to stare at her while he sipped his drink.

The entire evening was a living hell. He had never had to sit through anything this dull in his life. The food was frightful and if it wasn't for the drunk he was working on, the whole night would have been a write off. Shortly after eleven the room started clearing out and Shane glanced around, looking for Marren Lang. He had enough whiskey in him to nudge himself over to her and introduce himself. Maybe she would go out for a drink with him.

"You looking for Marren Lang?" his friend asked, coming up behind him. "She left about twenty minutes ago. I bumped into her as I was coming out of the john. I invited her over to the table to have a drink with us but she said she had an early day tomorrow and had to get out of this hole."

"So do I," Shane said, pounding back the remainder of his drink. "My flight leaves at nine."

His friend had given him directions for a short cut back to the slimy little motel he was staying at. Said he got them off a cab driver and that they would slice a good ten minutes off his trip. He wasn't drunk, but he sure as hell wasn't sober and could imagine driving around all night trying to follow the scribbled mess.

That's when it happened. He was at a red light and staring blankly out the windshield. Off to the left he saw a little burgundy hatchback parked over at the side of the street. A woman exited a small party store and was jogging back to the car, high heels clicking. Was it her? He couldn't be certain but she sure looked like her. Same black pants, same red hair, but a black blazer hid the top. Whoever she was, she walked around the front of the car and went to get in. That's when he heard a car's tires screeching, and a light blue Lincoln Continental squealed out of a parking lot across the street and raged toward her, hitting her.

"Fuck . . ." he breathed, jumping out of his rental car and rushing over to the woman's side. God dammit, it *was* her.

CHAPTER 5

She woke without the hangover she had the pleasure of experiencing the morning before. Thank goodness. That 'Juice' was like nothing she had ever had before. She was fairly well acquainted with alcohol but that stuff was just plain brutal. After the accident and the long recuperation her tolerance had dipped a bit, but her return to work reviewing bands raised it back up. The way Shane drank it, you would think it was mother's milk. He made it look easy. And it was. The 'Juice' would go down easy. It couldn't be described as *smooth*, not like an aged scotch, but it had a mollifying quality behind its lethal bite. The stuff had a friggin' personality, and a very likable one at that. The problem with it was that it had some pretty serious issues the next day. It was harsh and cruel. The angered one night stand. The bitter lover. Best call upon her again or you'll be sorry.

Again, there was a pleasant and homey breakfast, compliments of Mr. Helnsley, and another bright and sunny morning to appreciate. They had gotten far in their interview the night before, covering a good amount of material. They mostly talked about his work, focusing on several selected pieces. Marren had asked if he could explain some of the ways he utilized his words, and as she had a feeling he would, he cracked her up by becoming the old man in the blink of an eye. She found it hilarious to see this young and good-looking man speak the words of some profane old slimeball. There was no change in his deep and gruff voice, but his southern drawl became thicker and he pronounced his words in such a way that she couldn't help but laugh.

As repugnant as his responses were, the atmosphere around their work had taken on a light and comfortable feel. It was still exhausting, but as they became more and more comfortable with each other the tension in the work eased. Before they knew it, it was late – too late for them to rise for their fishing excursion in the morning.

It was that day and well into the afternoon when they realized that they had been working all morning and had missed the lunch hour. Shane suggested they actually pack up a couple of sandwiches and go have a picnic. The proposition made her bust out laughing. She asked if he was kidding and he insisted that he wasn't. Who went on picnics anymore? Weren't picnics for families and children? Company gatherings with three legged races and pie eating contests? You only saw men take women on picnics on television or at the movies. There were no men that actually did things like that . . . were there?

Apparently there were, and Shane was one of them, because before she knew it they were sitting under a tree about twenty feet away from the stream. They walked out to where the stream was a little wider and babbled good-naturedly over the rocks. Marren had aired her concerns about bears in the vicinity but Shane told her not to worry. He pointed out that aside from the tree they sat under, they were pretty much out in the open and would be able to see if any visitors were approaching. He had also toted along his rifle that he said "might not bring one down, but can be a real chum when it comes to scarin' one off."

"Killed many bears, have you?" she furthered.

"No. Not a one. No reason to. But if one is gonna come at me, I stand no chance unless I either scare 'im off or aim right for the heart."

The sun was hitting him just so, catching his hair and

showing off its color. It was a gentle brown but had a blond kiss to it. It looked like it would be amazingly soft to the touch and after a few hits from the 'Juice' bottle she found herself really wanting to just reach over and feel it.

He told her of the Athabascan people that called these areas home, showing her the necklace he had hanging around his neck. A young Athabascan girl from Dillingham had made it for him as a welcome when he moved up here. Myra was her name. Myra Meek.

Shane prodded her to tell him about her life down in St. Louis. He asked her if she liked it and asked her about her job reviewing bands. She felt hesitant to talk at first, not really knowing the man sitting in front of her, but then realized that she was staying in his home and would be for the next three and a half weeks. If that wasn't some kind of twisted trust, she didn't know what was. She permitted herself to open up to him, telling him that she felt her life was not what she had hoped it would be. "But give me time," she said. "I figure if I keep working for what I want, it'll come. Law of averages says so."

"What is it you want?" he asked.

"To want for nothing," she replied, without having to think about it.

"Money?"

"No. Not necessarily money . . . but peace," she said.

"This is as close to peace as your gonna get," Shane said. "This place, there's somethin' about it. It's thick with Spirit."

"You mean Alaska?" she asked.

"No. What Alaska does for the soul," he told her. "That's a place in itself."

"I don't think I could ever live the way you do," she smiled. "I like having a 7-Eleven close enough to grab a quart of milk or, better yet, a six pack, whenever I need it."

Shane smiled and shook his head. "You don't think you'd like living this way?"

"I dunno," she said. "Maybe if I had someone around that knew what they were doing. If I was alone I'd be lost. I'd be dead within a week."

God, she was beautiful. The sun was above and just behind her, casting a glow to her fire red hair that was lustrous and pleasing. She listened intently to everything he said to her but seemed reluctant to speak about herself too much. It didn't take long, however, for him to get her to volunteer some information about her life. A few questions and a few smiles, a little of Ed's truth serum and she was talking. She said that she wanted peace within herself and she seemed to think that success would bring her that peace. He wished she knew how dreadfully wrong she was. He had been there. He had lived it and it was the furthest thing from peace that he could think of. There was no spirit in success. No life. No spark. As green as success could be, it was gray underneath the surface. A lonely and ugly place.

She told him that someday her work would pay off and she would be where she wanted to be. How can anyone know where they want to be if they have never been there? He asked her that and all she did was give him a sly smile and say, "Tricky, tricky, tricky." He nodded, feeling entranced by her beauty and how it spilled over into her adorable words, but he didn't want his feelings to display themselves to her.

"Yeah, I'm tricky," he said.

"I know you are."

"What gave it away?"

"An educated man such as yourself shouldn't need to ask a question like that. You're just being tricky again."

"Educated," Shane laughed. "Yeah, that's what I am."

"You don't think so . . . Professor Helnsley?"

"No, I don't think so. Education is just having someone tell ya what you don't know. It's all out there *to* know. Ya just gotta open your eyes and look at it. I think the more ya look at, the more fucked up ya get. That's another one of the reasons I came out here. Got tired of lookin' around and taking in what I didn't need. All of this here – everything I got around me right this second – it's all I need."

The unspoken words in his mind and the crushing feeling deep in the core of his body were refusing to be ignored. If only he had the guts to reach out and touch her hand . . . if he could just lean over a little and kiss her. His mind began spiraling out of control. He imagined taking her in his arms and then laying her down on the blanket. He could practically feel her warmth under him as he fantasized about fumbling to remove her clothing, their hot heaving impassioned breath tangling between them. He could imagine running his hands over her skin, her breasts. It got so that the palms of his hands became sweaty and uncomfortably itchy with anxiousness. That's when he noticed that he had an erection and panicked. He glanced down to make sure it wasn't obvious, and thanked goodness the creases of his spacious work pants concealed his guilt. Regardless, the damn thing was throbbing and screaming out for service. It was going to have to be willed away. He swallowed hard and pulled in as much air as his lungs would hold as he grabbed for the bottle. He either needed to have her right now, or get a damn grip on himself.

Marren peered over at him as he helped himself to a charitable gulp of whiskey. He looked as if something had passed through him that could be compared to a demon. For a moment, he looked like someone that had just lived through a day packed full of broken alarm clocks, pink slips, forgotten house keys, credit collection notices, and a lingering and destructive case of heartburn.

"Is everything OK?" she asked, tilting her head down to get a glimpse of his face.

"Yeah, why?" He looked up at her.

"You look upset."

"No. I'm fine," he said, taking another hit from the bottle.

"I don't believe you. Do you hear a bear or something? Is something coming to eat us?"

Shane laughed, choking the mouthful of Juice up into his sinuses. Bears had been the last things on his mind. "No. We're not currently on the menu."

"Then what was it?"

"Nothing."

"Liar. What's wrong?"

"Christ, you're persistent," he chuckled, finding her tenacity charming. "Nothing is wrong. Cross my heart." He crossed his heart.

"Hope to die?"

"Sure. Yeah. Stick a needle, and all that shit," he said.

"I still don't believe you. You really looked like something was wrong."

There were dozens of things he wanted to say . . . *'Yeah, I fuckin' love you and I can't take you and it's killing me,'* and *'I want to make love to you so bad it physically hurts,'* and of course, *'I had a raging hard on thinking about jumping you and I was scared that it showed.'*

"I was just thinking about my agent," he finally lied.

"Is he giving you a hard time?"

"Not lately, which means he's due."

She nodded. He moved his gaze from the bottle to her and all those longing sensations revved up again, pinching, stroking and poking him in all the most inappropriate places.

She looked up at him and their eyes connected. He couldn't withstand much more of this and made an impetuous decision. He was going to risk it all and take her. Just reach over, touch her, kiss her and take her. Simply considering it, let alone making the decision and planning out the move, had him torturously excited. Then he visualized her pushing him away and slapping him across the face. His stare on her broke as he smiled, and then he laughed.

"What?" she asked, his smile causing her own to surface. "What's so funny? You're starting to give me a complex."

He shook his head. "Nothing."

His hair moved in the breeze as his laugh faded back into the smile. She felt a lump choke up in her throat and a pressure hit her in the chest. "You don't lie so well. Your smile gives you away," she said.

"Yeah, well . . . I've got a big nasty secret," he teased.

"I know you do. Now spill it."

His smile heightened into something cunning. "Make me," he teased. A man can hope. Surely a man can hope.

Marren rolled her eyes and snatched the bottle away from him. She took a hit and peered out at the stream. "It really is beautiful here, I'll give you that," she said.

"Yeah, it is," he agreed, his eyes still fixed firmly on her but not divulging what was really going on in his head. *It is beautiful here . . . especially today. Especially today.*

CHAPTER 6

'LT': *Do you have any plans on ever returning to Oklahoma?*

'SH': *Why would I wanna go back there? Ain't nothin' for me down there.*

'LT': *What about another book? Any plans for that?*

'SH': *Maybe. What 'ya gimme ta find out?*

'LT': *Well, this interview will give you a good medium to promote anything new you may be working on.*

'SH': *I was thinkin' more along the lines of workin' ya up on my lap, lil lady. See iffin I can't make ya squirm a bit.*

'LT': *Mr. Helnsley, surely you don't think that is appropriate to print here.*

'SH': *C'mon. C'meer and plop yerself down on 'ol grampy's . . .*

"Shane. I can't write this," she laughed.

"Why not. They all wanna know. They won't leave me alone until they do. The uglier it is . . . See, if we go all out and make me out to be the most repulsive human being alive, they'll leave me alone."

"But you're not repulsive. You're the furthest thing away from this old idiot and I don't feel right making you out to be this."

Shane dug deeply into her eyes. "What do you see in me, then? I wanna know."

"I . . . well, not this," she said, waving her notebook up in the air. "Definitely not this. Shane, what could be so bad out there that you can't face it?"

"Ya wanna know? Ya really wanna know?" he said, pushing his chair out with the backs of his knees and clomping heavily toward the counter to grab his bottle of Ed's Juice. "Fuckin' greed and anger and jealousy. People tryin' to kill each other. People always wantin' for themselves and never givin' a good God fuckin' shit for who they hurt."

She lit a cigarette and stared at him, sizing him up. He was ranting. She had obviously hit a nerve. Her words were calm. "That's not a good reason, Shane. Everyone has to deal with that."

He took his seat again. "I could do shit. I could work out a math problem in my head that would send a rocket into space and spit out an answer without even touchin' a piece of paper. I could memorize entire works of Shakespeare then explain it so a fuckin' monkey could understand it. They tested me and tested me until even the thought of thinkin' made me want to puke. I was pushed through school so fast it made my head spin and everybody wanted a piece of the little genius. Ferget playin' baseball or football or even watchin' Bugs Bunny. Everyone wanted to see me display my enormous fuckin' brain. I was a fuckin' circus freak . . ."

"Don't get upset," she said.

"I'm . . . I'm not," he said, collecting himself and lowering his volume. "I'm sorry. I wish I could help you understand, but if I did . . ." He stopped himself and stared at her for a moment before looking away.

"If you did . . . what?

"As a kid, that was enough, ya know? I thought it would all change once I was an adult, but it didn't. I saw someone I cared about get hurt, almost killed, and it meant nothing. Fuckin' nothing. Nobody could give a flyin' shit fuck about her, but they still had the time to beg my agent for a God damn morsel of my brilliance and a moment of my time."

"Who got hurt? May I ask?"

"It doesn't matter. Not now. But no one cared. I found that the only time I felt in any way comfortable was when I was writing and after I saw what I saw, my writing changed."

"It was her, wasn't it? The woman you talked about the other day. The one you love."

"Yeah. It's her," he said, tipping the bottle – the apparent life-blood that ran through his veins, flowing into his mouth. He kept his eyes on hers – dead serious. "My writing was to make me feel better. Not for the world of stuck up anal retentives and fashion sucking beatniks to chow down on. I felt like I was losin' my mind and I needed to get away from it. For good."

Marren was quiet. She had taken in everything he said and mulled it over, seeing that he meant business. "I'm sorry," she said, feeling a connection with him.

"I guess, in a way, I do understand a little."

"How's that?" he asked, having relaxed slightly from his emotional release.

"I was in an accident some years back and I almost lost my life. It took months for me to get back on my feet. It was hard. Really hard, but ya wanna know what kept me going?"

"What?" he asked, feeling his heart pound at the mere mention of the appalling crime he had witnessed.

"I don't remember it, but I was told that there was this man that saved my life. What you say, Shane, about people not caring . . . it's not true. This man that saved me, he cared enough to do it. They even told me that he called for months after, asking about me. I wanted to know who he was but they wouldn't tell me. They said that even they didn't know. He always said that he was just a friend."

Should he tell her? Jesus, he wanted to tell her. Should he? No. It would be too much and he had worked on this plan for too long to have it backfire in his face this early in the game. "You don't remember him at all?"

"No. I remember being at this stupid banquet as a favor to a friend of mine, but it all gets messed up in my head after that. Sometimes I think it's right there . . . ya know when you have a word right on the tip of your tongue . . . like that. Sometimes I see something that brings it on and I can almost get it, but it slips. It's maddening."

"I can imagine," he said.

"It's funny. Sometimes I'm glad I can't remember. See, I have this ridiculous image of that man in my head. He's like . . . perfect." She chuckled and gestured her hand out for a swig from his bottle, then she peeked up at him. "Sometimes I feel like I'm in love with him, but if I knew who he was all that would be destroyed. Stupid huh?"

"Shit, we're both comin' at it from two different directions, aren't we?"

"I guess we are. Look, Shane, I'm sorry. I didn't mean to question you."

His mind worked hard, breaking down all the possibles if he told her. 'God, I wanna tell her,' he thought. 'I wanna tell her and hold her in my arms and tell her I'm sorry. I'm so sorry no one cared. I'm so sorry I was the only one that stopped to help. I'm sorry I fell in love with you, but what else could I do? I'm sorry I think you're so agonizingly beautiful and I'm sorry I love you and I'm sorry no one ever cares.'

"Marren . . ."

"Mmm?"

"What would ya do if you knew him?"

"The man that saved my life?" she asked.

"Yeah."

"I'd thank him. I guess it's all I ever really wanted. Just to thank him."

He got up and opened a cupboard under the sink, pulling out another bottle of Ed's truth serum. Grabbing two glasses, he sat back down and poured them both a charitable amount. "I think we're gonna need this."

"If I'm getting up at four AM to learn how to fish, I think I should lay off of that stuff," she smiled.

"To tell ya the truth. I don't know what's gonna happen tomorrow," he said. He lit a cigarette and then placed his forehead in his palms. "Byron Dailey. That was his name."

"Pardon?" she asked.

"Byron Dailey," he repeated.

"Why does that sound so familiar?"

"That was the guy that the banquet was for," he said, sitting back and sighing.

Her eyes widened and her face had taken on an ashen hue. "What?"

"You walked in and I couldn't take my eyes off you. You were wearing black pants and this glittering top. Like you rode in on a blanket of stars. It had no back in it. You were beautiful."

"What are you talking about?" she asked, her eyebrows coming into a frown. She felt her stomach tighten into a queasy, horrified knot.

He covered his mouth with his smoking hand and spoke muffled but clear enough for her to hear him. "I was there. I'm him."

Her face had become pallid now. Bleached and panicked. "I . . . what . . ."

His heart was thumping so hard with what he feared he was doing that he could barely even hear himself speak. "You were getting in your car and this Lincoln came rippin' out of a parking lot and hit you. I saw it. I'm the one that helped you." The memory of it welled up in his gentle eyes and threatened to seep out, but he pressed his palms over them and halted the tears.

"You're him?" she asked, her voice having taken on a shaky and raspy tone as if she herself were holding back tears.

"I'm him," he confirmed, looking back at her and allowing her to see the thick sincerity spewing from his soul.

She stared at him for a moment, and all of a sudden her eyes grew to the size of dinner plates and tears rolled out of them silently. "Oh God. I remember. I remember you. It was you."

Shane again felt on the verge of tears himself. He got up and walked out into the living room, unable to face her. It wasn't shame. It wasn't fear. It was something so thick that he couldn't break through it to identify it. Whatever it was, it scared the shit out of him as it clawed at his heart, ripping it to jagged ribbons. If he had known that telling her was going to feel this way, he would have thought twice.

He knelt down by the fireplace and loaded a new batch of logs on the cradle as the sun was finally beginning to set. It must have been approaching ten PM. The house was quiet for the longest time and he hoped that he would find the courage to go back in there and look at her . . . but those tears, her tears, damn if they didn't stab at him and hurt him like he'd never felt before.

She remembered the face and she remembered thanking God for giving her something so wonderful to see before she died. At the time she believed that he was an angel, and had believed that to this day even though she no longer had the face in mind. Her guardian angel perhaps. The most handsome man she had ever laid eyes on and he had a kindness in his eyes of a like she had never seen before. Why hadn't he made himself known? Why did he . . . wait . . . What was going on? Shane

Helnsley, the poet. The guy asking her to lie for him. The man that requested her to write his story. What was going on?

Too much. It was too much to think about right now. She downed the rest of her glass and poured herself another and she wished she didn't learn what she had just been told. She stood up and went into the living room. "How do I know you're not lying?" she asked, sounding strong in between her sniffing.

He turned and looked up at her. "I'm not lying. I don't lie. It ain't my nature."

Again, another memory flooded back. He had said the same thing that night, didn't he? "Prove it," she challenged, not wanting to believe.

"He was your ex. Crazy fuck. Used to beat you. You got a restraining order on him and I guess it pissed him off. It was the corner of Washington and 21st, or close to. I called 911 but you stopped breathin' before they came. I gotcha back though.

"They told me that you had two surgeries. Your brain was really swollen and they had to release the pressure. That's why your left eye is a little lazy. You were in the hospital a bit more than four months and they called you 'the miracle.'"

She knew it was him. She remembered his face . . . Handsome. Gorgeous. "You could know all that from the papers."

"The night nurse that took care of you. Her name was Jennifer. She spoke with a lisp. That wasn't in the papers," he said. She said nothing. She just stared at him. His teeth bit into the inside of his cheek before he struck the last blow. "I paid your hospital bill."

Her posture noticeably changed from defiant and challenging to wilting. "Oh my God, it was you, wasn't it?" she said, remembering his face even more clearly now.

"Yeah," he swallowed.

"Why?"

"Because I had to."

"I didn't ask you to . . ."

"I know. You didn't need to."

"Why am I here?"

"I like your writing," he said.

"Bullshit!" she barked. "What is this? What kind of fucking weirdo are you?"

Shane turned back to what he was doing, striking a match and lighting the paper and kindling to get the fire going. "I'll have Ed come pick you up in the morning. Fly ya back out to Anchorage if ya want."

"That's it? That's all you have to say? You could at least just tell me what the fuck you had planned here."

"I'm sorry," he muttered.

"You're sorry? You're sorry. Oh, well that makes me feel a lot better. Drag me all the way up here handing me some crap about writing a story. Is Gavin in on this too? Jesus, just tell me the fucking truth. I need a good laugh. Tell me why I'm here, hero. Please!" Her tone was piercing and vicious.

He turned quickly and looked into her eyes, near cutting through her. "BECAUSE I FUCKIN' LOVE YOU, OK? I FUCKIN' . . . love you." He downed his glass and was quiet for a moment before adding, "And I do like your style. I do like your writing."

He peered back at her and her face looked strange. He couldn't read it and wasn't sure he wanted to know what it said anyway. Had he really told her? Had he really let that morbidly obese cat out of the bag? How could he be such an idiot? How could he be so impatient? He did not break his stare on her, nor did she look away from him, and a second later she broke out laughing. "You like my writing?"

He nodded his head just once. "Yeah, I do."

"And you love me, is that it?"

"Yeah," he affirmed.

She turned and walked back into the kitchen – back to her drink. She lit another cigarette, took her drink and headed out on to the back porch to get some air. It was getting dark and the first thing that popped into her head was the vision of her being attacked by a herd of rabid raccoons that reeked of garbage, frothing and snarling and shredding her to bits. The thought struck her as funny and then she realized that nothing here was funny. None of this was very funny at all. She had been tricked, lied to and made an ass of. Bastard.

He let her cool off out there, but sat in the kitchen to keep an eye on her. Make sure nothing came lumbering out of the woods. It wasn't all that uncommon and he'd be damned if he was going to let anything happen to her, even if she did hate him.

He had meant to make dinner but their work was on a roll and then this whole thing just happened, coming on without warning and now he had no appetite for anything but the juice. He doubted if she had any interest in a meal either. An hour had passed and it was nearing midnight. It had become quite dark out and he didn't want her sitting out there any longer. He downed his glass before standing up. He walked outside and stood just behind her.

"I want you to come inside. It ain't a good idea to be out here by yourself in the dark," he said.

"You call this dark?" she snickered.

"Marren . . ."

"I don't want to go in," she spat, sounding like the woman that she was but her words echoing those of a child's.

"Marren. I don't want ya out here by yourself. It's not safe."

"Oh, there ya go caring again," she mumbled.

"I'm serious."

"Then you come out here and protect me, like the big hero you are."

Arguing with her was obviously futile and he knew that picking her up and carrying her inside himself wouldn't go over very well. He went back inside, grabbed the bottle and his cigarettes and returned back to the porch. He sat down next to her, but kept his distance on the step above and behind her.

"Thank you for saving my life," she said quietly.

"I don't need you to thank me," he returned.

Was there anything he could say to her now that wouldn't cause more trouble? He doubted it and elected to just stay quiet. In the morning he would drive out to Dillingham and give Ed Lawry a call. It was very clear that Marren did not want to be here at this point. He could just give Ed a call, and ask him if he could spare a few hours and come get Marren to bring her back to Anchorage. Ed had warned him that this would happen if he didn't tread carefully, and Shane had agreed, but things had just exploded. He had been feeling like a shaken bottle of soda pop since she had arrived – like he would violently burst at any moment if dropped. And that's exactly what had just happened. The pressure behind his feelings was just too strong to endure and he simply exploded.

He thought getting away from everything would help, but it didn't. He just hadn't been feeling right. He hadn't outright lied to her, but he didn't tell her anything either. It was true, he had led her out here under false pretenses and why shouldn't she be pissed? The need for the story was there – that was not a lie – but he should have told her the truth up front and let her decide from there. Actually, he should have come forward years ago when she was in the hospital but the whole idea just seemed so crazy . . . 'Hi. My name is Shane Helnsley. I'm the guy that helped ya out the night you got mowed down by your psychopath ex. I'm the only one that stopped and gave a shit. Oh yeah, and by the way, did I mention that I'm the guy that is in love with you . . .?'

It was back then that he started to feel that he was cracking up. He didn't trust what was going on inside of his own mind, and what if he was wrong? What if his feelings toward her were just his snapping mind grasping out for something? He remembered back to the few weeks before leaving Oklahoma, bound for a solitary life in Alaska . . .

He was never one for teetotalling in the evening. He liked his drink, but more recently he found himself enjoying a three-drink lunch too many times to be deemed healthy. It didn't stop there, either. He had a bottle stashed in his office – strategically placed in the top right drawer of his desk. He felt like some kind of pathetic closet drunk after a week of that, and just started drinking it out of his coffee mug. Did that make it any less secretive? Any less shameful and wrong? No. All his students knew what was in the cup, and he didn't seem to care either way.

The sales of *Ugly People* was astonishing. Phenomenal. It was almost unheard of to see a collection of poetry such as his hit number one on the New York Times Bestsellers List. The amount of revenue it was generating was almost nauseating and feeding Shane's new affection toward the drink. He was still well liked and admired by his students but the Dean was starting to feel otherwise. He had a tendency to be nursing one helluva drunk by ten AM, and to be found sleeping it off during class. He was becoming infamous for staggering through the hallways and speaking gibberish about the impending collapse of humanity. It didn't matter though. He didn't need the job much at this point and the Dean knew it. Automatic job security. Shane was going to end up being wonderful publicity for the school. As he so typically put it to the Dean during one very unsavory meeting: 'any publicity is good publicity, you stupid old backfire spout of a man.'

So he liked his drink; it didn't seem to be affecting his performance as a professor. He was still pumping out dozens of literary genuises and achieving a class average of . . . well above average. So he wore a T-shirt and faded jeans under his sport coat . . . his now one and only sport coat since his other had been destroyed in St. Louis. So what? He was going to do the school a lot of good.

His agent started asking him to appear here and there. Signings and interviews. Talk shows and public engagements. Shane always blew him off. This is not what he had wanted, not at all. He hadn't wanted anything, in fact. All he had done was let his writing sway from its usual uniform and rule abiding spew to a prescription for his soul. Screw the rules, he had thought. Maybe he was losing his mind, but he couldn't get that astronomically beautiful woman in St. Louis out if it and it hurt like hell to not have her. Somehow, permitting the way he felt to seep through the end of his pen gave him some relief. There was no 'roses are red, violets are blue' bullshit, but tortured words of love and aching with a flavored dose of sheer anger and ulcerated views; punishing words unable to condone the behaviors of mankind. How can wild roses bloom from such iniquitous thorns? It was mad, he knew . . . so he drank to lull it. Hide it. Deny it.

It made money, however. Mounds and mounds of it. More than he knew what to do with. He had no desire to give into its pull. He was content to live in his small apartment. Content . . . that was a joke. He had been, or maybe it was just the calm before the furious shit storm. The few years he had away from the prying eyes of scientists wanting to put his adolescent and genius head in a jar for safekeeping was over. He was a man, on his own, with what he thought was a good job. A fulfilling job. Maybe even worthy of being labeled a career. God dammit, though, if he didn't feel as if he were under the microscope again and all from spilling his heart out onto a few pages. How could he possibly accept the vulgar rewards that had come from being a part of one very hideous night? Was it hideous? He had met an angel and how often does a man have the chance to do that? She was so absolutely beautiful that her image burned its way into his mind and controlled his every thought. How often does a man get to look into the eyes of an angel? At times he thought that perhaps looking into the eyes of an angel was a life sentence. That whole pillar of salt horse shit. Medusa and all that mythical jazz.

He had tried everything to stop thinking about her but nothing seemed to work. Hanging around in pubs and taverns getting so drunk he couldn't see didn't work. He only ended up with a hangover on top of the perpetual longing ache. Getting stoned didn't work either. Getting high only caused him to think unrealistic thoughts. Thoughts of possibilities that simply were not possible . . . not in this touch-to-feel world.

It was three AM on that one night when his spirit decided that clinging to this last thread would no longer do. His constant insomnia was beginning to get to him. He sat up in bed with a bottle of whiskey on the bedside table and a cigarette smoldering between his fingers. He looked over at the girl sleeping next to him in his bed. One of his students. Pretty girl. Young and firm. Bit of a dead-beat between the sheets, but who was he to judge? There was just no passion in it. She could have been wearing a paper bag on her head and it

91

would have made no difference. It was just the motions. Just a biological act. What was her name again? Was this the same one he was with last night? He didn't think so.

All his students. All lovely and young. All bright but probably looking for a good grade from the young genius professor that had long hair and wore jeans under his sport coat. His stomach tensed. Is this what life was going to amount to? Red pens, hands cracked and bleeding from chalk, fucking his students and feeling nothing? Fucking these nameless, faceless girls and hoping that his next drunken orgasm will knock the face of the angel out of his head? Jesus Christ . . . what the fuck was he doing? What the fuck was happening to him?

He got out of bed, pulled on his boxer shorts and went into the other room to call his agent. He had an idea that probably wouldn't go over very well, but it was the only way to save what he felt was left of his marbles.

Marren didn't know what time it was but the white glowing Alaskan blackness was really freaking her out. It was like black light and her eyes couldn't adjust to see anything properly. If it had not been for the dim light of the fire inside she wouldn't have even known Shane was sitting one step above and next to her. Once in a while she heard him take a swig from his bottle or light a cigarette and inhale it deeply.

However long it was that she had been out here, she spent it drifting back to her time recovering. It was a time she didn't like to revisit, but felt that she needed to so that she could decide what she was going to do about all of this.

Before tonight, she wasn't able to remember anything. Every now and then she would receive a fleeting picture of something but it was lost so fast that it felt more like déjà-vu than anything else. But tonight, when Shane told her it was him (her guardian angel she had spent the last few years thinking of and fantasizing about) it was as if the floodgates opened and she was still drowning in the first inexcusable swell.

Why in God's name did she agree to come to this ridiculous birthday banquet thing? Everyone in the room was such a friggin' tight ass. Drinking their champagne and speaking the praises of Myron, or Bryan or some such name. A poet . . . yeah, right. Marren had never heard of him but read one of his pieces out in the lobby of the banquet hall that had won some award. It was complete drivel. Fucking rhyming jabber, but oh so patterned and perfect in its unnecessary flow. Yeah, OK. She had laughed out loud when she read it and turned around with her friend to see everyone staring at them as if they had brutally murdered someone right there in the lobby. "That's no poem," she commented in a whisper. "It's a fucking douche ad."

There was the awards ceremony, which her friend didn't even win an award at, and then there were several speeches all dedicated to this Melvin guy, or whatever the hell his name was. Myron. Byron. Whatever. It went on forever and she was glad that she was at least able to order a real drink, or two . . . working on . . . whoops, ran out of fingers on that hand.

She was happy to be granted the forgiveness of her friend when she said that she really had to leave. She had a very early morning to look forward to and wanted to be somewhat alert for it. She headed for the lady's room first, and when coming out she bumped into an old acquaintance.

"Marren Lang . . . how are you?" he asked.

"Larry. Yes, hi. I'm good. How are you? I haven't seen you in ages."

"Can't complain. How's it at 'Room'?"

She scrunched her nose up. "Can complain, but it's a living, right?"

"Right, right," he chuckled.

She smiled a little. God, small talk was tedious.

"Listen, Marren, why don't you come over to my table for a drink. I got a friend of mine there that would really like to meet you."

"Oh, I can't. I really have to get going," she declined.

"Are you sure? He's a nice looking fella, or so the ladies say. Professor at Oklahoma State. Poet. Drinker. Smoker. Just your type."

"A professor? No thanks. I'm not into seniors quite yet," she smiled, backing away a step.

"No, no, no. He's twenty-nine. You've probably heard of him . . . Shane Helnsley?"

"Nope. Never. Look, I really gotta run. Early day tomorrow. Thanks though," Marren said, turning and making a quick exit.

There was a little tavern on North 21st that she liked to go sometimes. They made the best caesars in town, although all she wanted was a good hit of scotch. She took Washington, and as she was driving she reached into her bag and pulled out her cigarettes. Only one left. Shit. She would pick up a pack at the tavern but she hated those machines. Half the time they didn't work and you had to pester the bartender to get your money back.

Approaching 21st she pulled over to a small party type store to grab herself some more smokes. When she came out of the store and opened the door of her car there was a blunt thudding sound and then everything was just all over the place. She had fallen. Had she fallen? She remembered trying to get up, feeling terribly embarrassed and saying that she was OK. It was just her tripping over her own feet again. Yup

94

. . . first day with new feet, ha ha. But damn if she didn't all of a sudden feel like she'd been hit in the face with a sledgehammer. A twenty-pounder.

'Oh God . . . ' she thought. 'Oh God. I was hit by a car. Oh God . . . ' She then blacked out. When she came to, there was a man. A damn fine looking man, and he was hovering over her and wiping something off her face. Had she been sick? 'Oh, God, how humiliating,' she thought. 'No . . . it's blood. My . . . he's a pretty man. Why can you never run into these guys when you're at your best? Jeez, what I'd like to do to you . . .' All these thoughts swam through her fuzzy, soupy mind and she wanted to sort them out, hear them and understand them. But she was so tired. So very tired.

A beeping noise woke her up and an oddly displaced sound of swooshing. She opened her eyes – which took a hell of a lot of work – and turned her head to see that she was in a large dimly lit room. Green walls. Pale green. She wondered if she was dreaming about life as a big woozy feeling breath mint. As she woke up a little further, she realized she was in a hospital. Her throat hurt like hell and she tried to swallow, but ' . . . Jesus, there's a tube down my throat.' The swooshing sound was a machine pumping air into her body through the fucking tube.

There was a whole shitload of tubes as a matter a fact. Out her nose, her hand, her arms. The nurse rushed over and calmed her down, telling her everything was OK. "Just take it easy. Relax," she said. Marren reached up and grabbed at the tube in her mouth and began yanking at it. The nurse told her to stop, to calm down . . . "It's there to help you breathe," she said, gently grabbing Marren's wrist and then checking the tube.

"Geh iss fuccckin' singg outta muh-ee!" Marren barked, pulling it halfway out and gagging on it.

95

"Shhhh. Miss Lang, you shouldn't do that," the nurse said, her eyes huge.

Another nurse came along and looked Marren over. "You don't want it?"

"Uhh uhh," Marren sounded her disapproval.

"OK," the second nurse said. "Hold still," she said, taking the tube and gently pulling it out.

Marren gagged again and then coughed. Her throat was so sore and dry she couldn't stand it. She tried to swallow but there was nothing to swallow. Her lips felt like corrugated cardboard and her tongue felt like a big wadded up piece of fleece stuffed in her mouth. "Can I have a drink?" she whispered.

"You can have some ice chips, OK?" the nurse said, spooning one in her mouth and looking up at the other nurse. "Go get Doctor Bastien . . . fast."

"Am I sick?" she asked.

"Yes, Marren. You are, but you're getting better."

"What's wrong with me?" she rasped. "I feel like shit."

Just then an elderly doctor stepped up next to her bed as the nurse began to take her blood pressure. He smiled at her. "Hi there. I'm Doctor Bastien," he said. "How are you feeling?"

"Like shit," she repeated, in a hoarse mumble.

"Well, that's to be expected. You have been through quite an ordeal."

"What ordeal?"

"You were hit by a car and sustained some very serious injuries," the doctor told her, looking into her eyes with a little penlight. She squinted away from it.

"Am I OK?" she asked, again, looking for something to swallow to ease her dry throat. The nurse gave her another few ice chips.

"I'd say that so far everything is coming along nicely," he answered.

What kind of answer was that? The kind of answer you give someone that was pretty fucked up, that's what kind of answer that was. She willed herself to move her fingers and her toes and found that she could, but the movement hurt in a stiff kind of way. She could feel her legs . . . everything. So . . . what, then? "Tell me why I'm here. What's wrong with me?"

"Do you know your name?" he asked.

"Course I know my name," she hissed.

"What is it?"

"Marren Lang," she answered.

"How old are you?"

"Why? Have I lost any time?" she came back.

Bastien pursed his lips. "Just over a month."

She sighed with relief. A month was a long time, but it was better than being told a year. "I'm twenty-six."

"Do you know what year it is?" he asked.

"Yeah. 1996," she replied.

"Very good. Now let me ask you, do you remember anything about the accident?"

Marren blinked and shifted in the bed a bit, finding her body so stiff and painful she cringed. "No. Was my car totaled?" she asked.

"No. Your car is just fine. Just lost a door. Marren . . . it was a hit and run and you alone were hit, and quite hard I might add. You had five broken ribs, a punctured lung, a shattered ankle, a broken collar bone, and a very serious head injury."

"Jesus . . ." she breathed. "That's why I feel like shit."

"Yes, that's right," he smiled faintly.

"Head injury? I'm thinking OK, aren't I?"

"Yes. You're thinking just fine. That's good to know. You

see, you hit your head very hard and it caused some bleeding and bruising. Your brain swelled up quite a bit and we had to release the pressure by making a small opening in your skull . . . right here," he said, pointing to an area on the back of his own head.

"There's a hole in my skull?" she asked.

"Well, there was. For drainage and the release of pressure, but we put you all back together again. It'll take a while to heal up, but it looks to me like you're going to do just fine." He was happy with all her vital signs and babbled some medical jargon to the nurse before looking back at her. "By the way, Marren. When you were brought in you were asking for someone named Shane. Is this your boyfriend, because we can't find him?"

"Who?" she asked.

"Shane."

"No. I don't know any Shane," she answered.

"OK, well, good enough. Now you get some rest."

Rest, yes. She had just woken up after sleeping for over a month, but she was exhausted. She had wanted to get up, get dressed and get out of there, but every fiber of her being was about as able as a newborn. Just speaking with the doctor had her feeling as though she had run a marathon. She tried to lift her head off the pillow to a more comfortable position, but couldn't. Her muscles were unwilling. She then attempted to reach up to feel the area of her head that Bastien had told her about, but her arm felt like it was not only strapped to the bed, but filled with warm liquid lead. As much as she could, she shifted around to where the sheets felt cool under her skin, and slipped back into sleep.

She was transferred from ICU into a room of her own within a week, surprising even Bastien. She then spent the next two months getting back on her feet. Physical therapy every damn day. It was excruciating, frustrating, discouraging and terribly humiliating. She wasn't alone during her therapy – there were others fighting to regain movement and control of themselves as well, and some that appeared much worse off than herself. The repeated failure was, however, overwhelming at times. More than once she would be depleted to the point of tears, which only made everything seem more hopeless. There she would be, grasping two metal bars, her useless legs and ankles bent in unnatural ways refusing to hold her weight and dangling below her. She would drag them behind her as she pulled herself forward, allowing herself to feel some level of accomplishment for having regained the strength in her arms, but she was always reprimanded for not trying to use her legs.

"C'mon, you can do it, Marren. You've proven that with our exercises."

"I can't," Marren bumbled, looking down at useless twigs that hung there so pathetically weak.

"Yes, you can."

"No, I can't."

"Marren, yes you can."

Marren peered up at her therapist, the parental look on his face only feeding her anger. "I hate you!"

"I know you do. That's OK. Now, try it again."

Then there was the hospital food. They tried to keep a varied menu, but after being a resident for as long as she had been, she began to enjoy the tedious weekly pattern. Monday's salsbury steak looked like one of those novelty store rubber shits, and tasted like one too. Tuesday's fried chicken – dry, tasteless, and . . . gray. Every entrée served with a side of springy freezer burn vegetables and some kind of potato product, be it dehydrated mashed (just add water), hash browns, or french fries. And then there was dessert.

Pudding every second day – rice, vanilla and chocolate, and Jello every other day – red, green, orange, red, green, orange, and so on.

During her stay, she had become an expert on the topic of soap operas, seen three different room-mates come, get healthy and go, and completed two hundred and thirty-six crossword puzzles. She was thankful when Bastien felt she was up to being questioned by the police. It was a very welcome and refreshing change in routine.

Approximately two weeks after she was questioned, she learnt that her ex-boyfriend, David Spelling, had followed her from the banquet hall that night and ran her over. He apparently told the police that she deserved to die. Lovely. Just lovely. She was hoping that the restraining order she had against him might have spooked him at least enough to leave her alone. Who was she kidding, right?

The night nurse from ICU came to visit her everyday after she left. Jennifer. Sweet lady. Had trouble pronouncing her S's. She told Marren that she had a secret admirer.

"Who? What are you talking about?"

"Thome nithe man callth every other day to thee how you're doing. I know all the nurtheth on our floor wouldn't thtand for it, tho I had the callth bumped up to me."

"What's his name?" Marren asked.

"Don't know. Thayth he'th jutht a friend."

"It's not a guy named David Spelling, is it? That's my ex. He's the bastard that did this to me. Put me in here. He tried to kill me."

"No," Jennifer said. "Haven't you heard?"

"Heard what?"

"He'th going away for a real long time. Read it in todayth paper. No. Thith ith thomeone elth. Thoundth really hot . . . and he really liketh you."

The fun didn't stop once she was released from the hospital. She had small blanks in memory here and there, but the doctor said to expect it and that it would all come back in time. First and foremost on her mind, however, was the hospital bill. She didn't have insurance at the time of the accident and was regretting it now. She had always meant to get herself some coverage, but it was one of those things that she kept putting off.

Daily she would check her mail for the bill, but it never came. Due to her problems with memory, she would check around her apartment looking for it, wondering if it had come and she had forgotten about it. After a few weeks of waiting, checking, and going through every scrap of paper in her apartment, she called the hospital. She was put on hold three times, each time causing her more anxiety. The amount due was going to be a fortune. How the hell was she ever going to pay it?

"Accounts receivable?" a voice finally said.

"Yes, hello. My name is Marren Lang and I'm checking into the status of my recent bill. I've not received it yet."

"Hold please."

Marren sighed, but the voice came back on quickly. "What was that name?"

"Lang. Marren Lang. I was there . . ."

"Your bill is paid in full, Ms. Lang."

Marren frowned. "Excuse me?"

"This bill is paid in full."

"That's not possible. I didn't pay it. Who . . ."

"It is paid, Ma'am. A copy of the invoice will be sent to you before the end of the month, for your records."

Marren was quiet for a moment, then asked for clarification. "Are you sure?"

"Yes Ma'am."

"Who paid it?"

"It doesn't say here, Ma'am . . ."

"Well isn't there a cancelled check or something . . ."

"It's on file as being paid cash, Ma'am."

"Cash? What?"

"Is there anything else Ma'am?"

Marren chewed on her lip. "Um . . . no . . . I guess not."

She called her boss and asked if he had paid it, and he laughed. "I felt horrible for what happened to you, Marren, and I want you to get well, but I didn't pay your hospital bill for you. Where would I get that kind of money?" She thought of David, her ex, but first of all he was in jail, and second of all, that freeloading prick didn't have any money. Who else could it possibly be?

She took another month before going back to work, knowing that the last thing she needed was a loud rock band to blow through the just recently repaired hole in her skull. Once she was back to work, though, it didn't take long to swing back into her old routine, and that included her fondness for a few drinks. Hell, if it were possible, she found that her tolerance had gone up. Must've been all the morphine she had been on for the first few weeks had made the alcohol mere oatmeal to her system. Well . . . that was her theory anyway.

A couple of years passed and although she couldn't explain it, she couldn't get that man off her mind. The man that had saved her. She didn't know him. She couldn't remember him. But she and Jennifer had put two and two together to realize that whoever the guy was that witnessed the accident and saved her life was the same guy that had called to check up on her. Jennifer suggested that she call the police and ask them who he was. They might be able to tell her. It was a good idea, but Marren decided not to bother trying. She kind of liked the idea of having an admirer that she didn't know. It made it a little more romantic and he could look exactly the way she would like him to look. Silly, yes, but after what she had gone through, the thought of having a man around didn't sit well with her. It was bad enough that she could sometimes almost remember him. Little things. A white T-shirt. A southern drawling accent. A good smell. A smile and a joke . . . something about a goose egg, but she could never quite grasp it and decided that she probably never would. That was fine. Better that way, in a way.

She would find herself daydreaming about this man. She would let herself believe that he was this ruggedly gorgeous thing that would be able to take her breath away. At times she believed that she was in love with him, or at least the idea of him, and this was comforting to her. It preoccupied her a lot of the time, which was a pain in the ass, but it was also always pleasant. Hell, the whole thing had the makings of another novel, but she really didn't want to try that again. It was nothing but a huge failure the first time around and had lost its appeal.

And so, here she sat in the Alaskan dark, next to Shane Helnsley. The man that saved her life. Her guardian angel. The secret admirer with the generous purse strings. The famous poet that had tricked everyone . . . and now he had tricked her. Still, it was curious. He was curious. A curious man to say the very least.

He had said that he loved her, but how was that possible? She had never met him in her entire life, nor had he ever met her. The night was cold and she shivered but didn't want him to see that she had. There were noises off in the woods that were eerie, but she held her ground. "You said you loved me.

Did you want to explain that to me?" she suddenly said after the expanse of silence.

"It'd take me too long, if I even could," he said.

"We have all night, and I'd really like to know," she countered.

Off in the brush there was a rustling sound and Shane sat up a little straighter. "Come inside," he said quietly.

"I . . ." she attempted, not having noticed the movement.

He took her by the arm. "Come inside. We have a visitor."

"OK," she said, not about to argue and standing up with him.

Inside, Shane kept the lights in the kitchen off. He crept over to the side window and peered out. "There she is," he whispered.

"Who? There who is?" she begged, feeling nervous.

"The Cinnamon Black I told you about. Come here. Don't ya wanna see her?"

Marren moved toward him and he put his arm around her and urged her next to him to look out the window. She could barely see anything, just darkness. "I don't . . ."

"Right there by the shed," he whispered next to her ear.

She squinted in the direction he had told her and there she was. She was huge, or as big as any bear she had ever seen. The unfamiliar lighting of the night sky in these parts, and the hazy kind of moonlight, lit the bear's back, showing off the orangey glow of her coat. As magnificent as she was, Marren felt terrified and her shoulders reacted by shrinking inward. Shane placed his mouth up close to her ear. "It's OK. She comes around a lot. She's just lookin' around. Don't worry. She'll smell that we've been around and she'll leave. Always does."

His breath through her hair was near erotic. She could

pick up on the warm scent of the whiskey on his breath and it sent a sensual chill up her spine, like she wanted to taste it from him. With his arm around her shoulder he was close and the heat off his body couldn't be ignored. A moment earlier she was feeling rather petrified that a monstrous bear was hulking its way around outside the house, but now she was being taken over by another, and rather unwelcome, feeling; she liked the way Shane felt. That was, indeed, unwelcome.

He kept his mind first and foremost on the bear, but Marren was so close and she smelled so good. Like lilacs on a moist spring wind. Her hair was as soft as silk on his lips as he whispered to her and her small frame felt unbelievably pleasing next to him.

"How long do we have to stand here, like this?" she whispered, wanting to get away from him and the sensation she was feeling which was now nearing delighted pins and needles. Indeed unwelcome.

He took his arm away. "Don't have to. I just thought you'd wanna see her."

She quietly moved out of the kitchen and went and sat by the fireplace. He had failed. He knew. She would never be his. She would never accept this God damned love he wanted to give her, and she would never return it. He'd made a mistake.

He grabbed his bottle and joined her out in the living room, sitting on the sofa as he had the night before. They sat quietly for a while, before she spoke up. "Can we talk a little more about this?" she said, keeping the volume of her voice low.

"Sure," he said.

"You never answered my question."

"No. You're right. I didn't."

"Are you going to?" she asked.

"Why don't you tell me what you'd like to hear and I'll do my best to comply," he muttered.

"No," she said. "Why don't you tell me the truth?"

His eyes shifted from the fire to her. Her beauty. God, was she really gonna make him do this? Yes, she was. "I liked your book," he started and Marren tried not to laugh out loud at his words for fear of the bear outside. He continued. "I didn't want to go to that fuckin' dinner. Byron's big birthday party. I don't know why I accepted the invitation, I hardly knew the guy.

"You walked in and the whole room just disappeared. I don't know why, it just did. I watched you all night and I really meant to go over and introduce myself, but before I knew it, you had left.

"I had to catch a flight the next morning so I left too. Larry, my friend Larry, gave me a quicker route to my motel. Down Washington. Down 21st and so on. That's when I saw what happened.

"When I looked into your face, something just hit me. I wish I could explain it, but I can't. Jesus, Marren . . . I just . . . I fell in love with you. I know I'd never even met you and I wasn't sure if I was losing my mind or not, but I know now that it's true. After meeting you and having you around, I know now. I love you."

She said nothing and he felt like he had to go on . . .

"I'm sorry I didn't come forward back then, back when it happened. I'm sorry I wasn't honest with you right up front, but hey, look at the bright side . . . ya got to see Alaska." He stared at her, her expression flat and cold, her eyes squinting a rage just under the surface. "I'll drive into town first thing tomorrow and call Ed to come on out here and pick you up."

Through his speech Marren felt those old familiar emotions hit her. All the day-dreaming about the stranger that saved her life. That's when the realization hit her. She had imagined him as this gorgeous man . . . and God dammit, he was. She had imagined him taking her breath away and sweeping her off her feet . . . and God dammit, he could, and was.

"This is ludicrous," she blurted out.

Shane sat back, feeling defeated and wondering how much juice would heal his pride, while taking a hit. "Yeah, well . . . people say I'm crazy. You know that."

She stood up. "I think I'm just going to go to bed. That bear isn't gonna come hurtling through the window in there, is it?"

Shane shook his head no and she left him.

CHAPTER 7

She wrote quickly, almost automatic scribbling, her hand guided by her anger at being deceived.

> 'Helnsley has bribed and bought his way out of the public eye. His desire to be left alone can only be deemed as selfish and insecure. His views on everything in our society are overblown and completely unreasonable. If any of the rumors about Helnsley are true, the ones of his mental competence, or lack of, are.
>
> 'He spends his days fishing, chopping wood, bear watching, drinking and allowing everyone to believe that he is something other than what he really is, while the bucks roll in. Unwilling to do any of the footwork that would justify a success such as his, he smiles at the fact that we've all been had.'

She sat on the bed, gazing over at the pot belly stove in the corner, remembering all the things he had said to her. She was angry, but that anger seemed muted. Stifled. She wanted to continue writing but she was too shaken up. The little bit she had put down had appeased her desire to hurt him in return. She put her notebook back in her bag and covered it with a T-shirt.

She pulled her jeans off and crawled in under the covers, clicking off the lamp next to her. As on the nights before, she left the door open a crack because after what she had seen in the back yard tonight, she didn't feel as safe as she would have liked. She knew he was out there in the living room, not thirty feet from where she lay, and it made it hard for her to close her eyes.

Tomorrow, she could finish her article on the plane. That is, if she was even able to get a flight out of Anchorage at the last minute. Still, a nice hotel room with a mini fridge and a television set sounded good. She could lie around all evening and write if there were no flights available.

That bastard.

Shane took his shirt off and lay back on the couch. He wasn't drunk, but he wasn't sober. Why did his body always find this sickening middle ground no matter how much he drank? Didn't matter. Ed had restocked him just before Marren arrived and he had enough juice to put him into a coma if he had the energy to drink it all. Three bottles down, twenty-one to go. God bless that man, Ed Lawry. When he spoke to him in the morning he would be sure to invite him up for a weekend of fishing and boozing in the very near future. That would be fine. Get his mind off things.

He knew she was in there, not thirty feet away from him, and the pain in his chest was near insufferable. He shouldn't have told her. How could he be so fucking stupid? He remembered her standing at the window in the kitchen. God, the way she felt up close to him like that. Her hair. Her . . .

'Forget it,' he thought. 'Just have another drink and forget it. It's over.' He tipped the bottle and poured a couple of good shots into his mouth, practically opening his throat and allowing it to just slide right down. He put the bottle on the floor and closed his eyes. Sleep. Sleep would help and tomorrow he'd get her out of there and he could go back to the way things were. Nice and uncomplicated. He would have to forget about her first, but how hard could that be? He could just forget about her and all of this.

110

* * * *

She was restless and her sleep was sketchy. When she lay awake all she could think about was what had happened and how the man she had been so preoccupied with for years was right there. In her little spurts of sleep were dreams of the ICU. The old and hopeless cases and the young and broken victims, each of them tragic. Also in that mint green room and all around her, was him, Shane, just under the surface, caring about her, and all she wanted was to know him, thank him, and be held by him.

What time was it? It had to be early – or late, depending on how you looked at it – because the sun was coming up. There was no way of knowing what time it was. No clock in the room. The fire in the stove wasn't out but had burned down quite low. The room itself was warm and felt like a big cozy sweater around her as she sat up in the bed. She peered across the room toward the door that still stood open a crack. The fire in the living room had not gone out either and its light glowed and moved in strange flickering shadows through the increasing morning light.

"Aren't you going to teach me how to fish?"

Shane woke to see Marren sitting on the floor right next to the sofa, her hand on his arm. He didn't know up from down for a moment and gathered his bearings. He pulled his other arm out from between himself and the back of the couch – it had fallen asleep – and looked at his watch. "It's three forty-five," he mumbled. The events of the previous evening then became clear in his numb mind. She didn't seem to have anything to say about the time, prompting him to sit up. "What are ya doin' out here?" he asked.

"I think I owe you an apology," she said.

"No ya don't," he said rubbing his face. "You don't owe me anything."

111

"You saved my life. You paid my hospital bill. You cared. You're him," she said. "I always wanted just to know who you were."

"Yeah, well . . . don't worry about it. I did my good deed."

She stared at him and he stared back. She gave him a small smile but it faded off her face as quickly as it had appeared. Lifting herself up slightly on to her knees, she leaned over and kissed his cheek, then pulled away slowly. It was a soft kiss. Not a quick peck, but warm and sensual.

The next few moments were torturous. She didn't know what to say or do and he looked like he didn't either. Should she just pick herself up off the floor and go back to bed?

She didn't even see it coming even though his movements were unhurried and fluid. He reached up and placed his hand gently around the back of her neck, urging her to come back to him. He kissed her sweetly on the lips and so softly that had she been standing up, her knees would have buckled and she would have just fallen right over. She didn't fight him. She didn't fight what he was doing, but permitted it, and his kiss didn't stop at one. Once he felt secure that what he was doing was alright, he followed it up with a second, then a third.

She wanted this. It felt good and right. The memory of his face that night of the hit came at her in waves and he felt this approval in the way she was kissing him back. It fueled his passions and he persuaded her up from her kneel with encouragement from his hands, easing her from the floor up on to his lap. Her legs over the top of his thighs, he kissed her with a desire that she had never experienced before.

He gently rubbed his hand down her side, over her hip and on to her thigh, then stopped kissing her and looked down. "Long johns?" he smiled, looking down at her legs and then back up to her face.

She smiled back. "It's cold up here," she defended.

She could barely get the words out of her mouth before his amused smile was kissing her again. The calenture between them heightened with each touch of their lips and tongues. Shane covered her neck in kisses, letting her scent push him as far as he could go without losing his control altogether. He picked her up in his arms and carried her through the living room and into the bedroom, where he placed her down on the bed.

He watched her undress in the thickening morning glow, the only other light coming from the glass window of the stove. She was more beautiful than he had ever imagined and he found himself staring at her stupidly for several long moments before getting out of his pants and lying down on top of her, taking her in his arms.

After making love intensely they fell asleep in each other's embrace without uttering a word about what had just transpired. For Marren, she knew exactly what she was doing when she wandered out into the living room to wake him. She didn't *really* want to go fishing. Fishing had nothing to do with it, it was simply the perfect way to wake him and that was all. When she saw him there sleeping, she knew he was indeed the man she had envisioned for the past three years. If it were possible, he was more, and she decided that it was forgivable to want to be close to him.

For Shane, speaking would only disturb the poetry that had just taken place in his arms. There would be plenty of time for talking later. All he wanted was to feel her life held close to him. He wanted very much to tell her he loved her again, but thought it would be redundant if not dangerous right now. He was holding her and he didn't want to do or say anything that might change that perfection.

The sun had risen completely and seemed to reflect off the

snow and ice on the distant mountain tops, shimmering down into the clearing. They had been awake for a little while, making love for the second time and relishing it. It was unspoken but mutually understood that Shane would not be driving into Dillingham to place a call to Ed Lawry that day.

He aired his desire for a cigarette and Marren pointed at her pack on the tiny table next to the bed. He picked it up to find that it was empty and wondered where the hell he had left his the night before. "I have an open carton right there in my bag," she said.

He leaned out of the bed, needing to brace himself with a hand on the floor and reached over, pulling the bag closer. A T-shirt slid off the top and right there in front of his face was her open notebook. He rummaged for the carton while his eyes skimmed over the first several lines . . .

'This interviewer has a truth to share that you may find shocking.

'We have all been tricked and made fool of. The hideous and perverse old man that was believed to be Shane Helnsley is nothing more than an invented character, created by Helnsley himself, to protect himself from the prying eyes of the world.

'The handsome thirty-three year old man resides approximately twenty miles north of Dillingham, Alaska, in a house he built himself. A sanctuary . . .'

He picked it up and held it up for her to see. "What the hell is this?" he asked.

Marren's eyes focused on the book and her heart sank. "Shane . . ."

"Is this what you're planning on printing?" he furthered, turning the page and reading out loud . . .

"Helnsley has bribed and bought his way out of the public eye. His desire to be left alone can only be deemed as selfish and insecure. His views on everything in our society are overblown and completely unreasonable. If any of the rumors about Helnsley are true, the ones of his mental competence, or lack of, are."

"Shane . . . I . . ."

He kept his eyes on the page but held up his hand to silence her. He continued . . .

"He spends his days fishing, chopping wood, bear watching, drinking and allowing everyone to believe that he is something other than what he really is, while the bucks roll in. Unwilling to do any of the footwork that would justify a success such as his, he smiles at the fact that we've all been had."

He tossed the notebook on to her lap. "Is this what you think?" he asked, hardly able to believe the words he had just read. "This is what you think of me. Shit . . ." he breathed, climbing out of the bed and pulling his pants on. "Was I ever wrong about you."

"Don't say that, Shane. Shane . . ." she attempted, but he left the room.

She scrambled off the bed, quickly throwing her own clothes on, and rushed out of the room after him. She found him with his shirt on already and pulling his boots on. "Shane . . . I . . ."

"What was last night, Marren? Needed somethin' else to write about?"

"No. Shane, I . . ."

"Don't bother," he blurted, grabbing the bottle that still sat next to the sofa and heading for the back door.

"Shane, please. Stop. I just don't think it's fair to leave everyone in the dark like you've been doing."

"I'll send Ed out to get you. Be packed up and ready by noon. I won't be back 'til after you're gone. I can't look at you," he finished, walking out the door, slamming it behind him.

She stood in the bedroom doorway for a second longer, then hurried over to the window and looked out to see Shane take off in his truck like a maniac. Headed for what road, she didn't know. She hadn't seen any roads around on their walks. He just drove out across the clearing until she couldn't see him any more.

She didn't know what to make of what just happened and dropped herself down into one of the kitchen chairs and started to cry. Selfish, she had called him. Who was really being the selfish one here? Was it wrong to want to succeed? Would it really be so God awful if everyone knew the truth about him? None of this had crossed her mind as he made love to her the night before and that morning. All that was going on in her mind was a desire stronger than she knew how to cope with. It was crazy, but she swore she had fallen in love with him. "Son of a bitch," she mumbled through her tears. "I am. I'm in love with him."

As she packed up her things she wished as hard as she could that he would come through the door and forgive her, but he didn't. At noon she went to sit on the front porch, ready, just like he said. It wasn't until one-fifteen that she heard the engine of a plane approach. It zoomed over the clearing, circled around and landed fifty yards away from the house.

Marren wiped the tears off her face, gathered her bags and started walking toward the Cessna. Ed had gotten out and opened the door for her, giving her a polite but emotionless smile. He closed the door behind her and as he did, Shane's truck pulled up next to the house. Marren's heart pounded with a sick kind of excitement, hoping that he had changed his mind.

Ed turned to see him and the two walked through the clearing to meet each other half way. They talked for a few minutes and occasionally Shane would look over at the plane . . . and her inside. He gave no indication that he had had a change of heart and she felt her own heart break into a million pathetic pieces as they shook hands and Shane walked back to the house.

Her eyes watched him. God he was beautiful and she could still feel his arms around her. His kisses on her lips. She could still hear his voice, his accent, and she wanted to smile from it but choked down a sob instead. He didn't turn around but went back inside without so much as a glance.

He lit a cigarette and watched through the front window as Ed took off. He felt like he just wanted to cry, but he didn't. He had made a mistake and the pain he was feeling was just part of the learning process. The dull ache that would swell in crushing waves was there to let him know just how bad a mistake he had made.

He walked into the bedroom, pulled the sheets off the bed and took them out back. He dropped them in a pile on the fire pit, doused them with gasoline and dropped a match on them.

"Did he say anything?" Marren asked, breaking the agonizing silence in the plane.

"Shane? 'Bout you?" Ed asked.

"Yes," she said quietly but loud enough to be heard over the engine.

"Well," he started. "I don't usually make a habit of betrayin' a friend's confidence, and Shane is a good friend."

"I understand," she muttered.

Ed glanced over at her. "You hurtin' over him?" he asked.

She nodded. "Yeah," she said, but no sound came out.

"Well, he's hurtin' too. Ms. Lang, don't print what ya wrote about him. Don't do that to him. He doesn't deserve it."

She didn't reply, but wiped her face again.

Nothing was said again until they landed in Anchorage. Marren climbed out of the plane and before she made her way into the airport, Ed called after her. "He loves you, ya know. Shane does."

CHAPTER 8

He spent that day re-evaluating his idea of what being drunk really was. Toward evening he came to the conclusion that he had been dreadfully misinformed and that a proper drunk, a respectable drunk, didn't stop at just drunk. That first night after she left he downed three bottles of Ed's juice only to throw it all back up again. As he heaved off the side of the back porch he was relieved to find another thought in his head other than *her*. *'What a waste.'* he thought as he retched. *'Now I gotta start drinkin' all over again.'*

During that first week, he seemed to have forgotten to eat and shower and change his clothes and go anywhere near the bedroom. Well, the latter was being avoided rather than forgotten. The other thing he had forgotten was that he inadvertently told Ed to pop by for a good drunk next chance he got. Ed was usually bogged down with flights all over the place and Shane really didn't expect to see him any time soon.

It was that first Saturday after Marren left that Ed showed up on his doorstep. *Showed up on his doorstep?* How could you not notice that Ed was around? That friggin' Skylane of his wasn't something you pulled up into the driveway inconspicuously.

Shane opened the door and welcomed him with a "Hey buddy!" and a very obvious stagger.

The fumes of alcohol that emanated off of Shane were ferocious. Ed peered down at the cigarette between his fingers and was actually surprised that he hadn't already burst into flames. As he stepped passed him he also picked up on the scent that suggested his friend hadn't been in the shower for a while. "You drunk, Shane?"

"Course I'm drunk," he said, and then laughed.

Ed snatched the bottle out of Shane's fist and took a hit himself. "Not doin' very well, I see."

"I'm doin' just fine, Eddie," Shane said, clomping across the living room and sitting down on the sofa.

Ed glanced over at the desk and saw a fresh batch of poetry scattered all over the desk. Along with the papers were four empty juice bottles and two ashtrays overflowing with butts. "Been writin'?"

"Have I?"

Ed wandered over to the sofa and crouched in front of him, eyeing him. "Shane, you're a fuckin' mess. Ya stink. You're a week's drunk and . . ."

"I'm fine," Shane said, his head weaving in a small circle with his words. "I don't stink, do I?"

"No, you're not fine. Jesus, I sure as hell didn't expect to find ya like this. I knew you were upset but . . ."

"Upset?" Shane laughed. "I love her. I've loved her for years and I . . ." he stopped.

"What?" Ed asked, egging him on to let it out.

"I had her in my arms. I had her. God, right here," he confessed, holding himself around his middle. He let himself go and stared at Ed for a moment, then he buckled over his lap and began to weep.

"Christ, Shane . . ." Ed breathed, putting his hand on Shane's shoulder. "Ya love her that much?"

Shane straightened up and grabbed the bottle back from Ed. He scrubbed at his face with his hand and contained himself. "Yeah," he grunted. "I love her that fuckin' much."

"Go take a shower. I'll fix ya something to eat and we'll talk, OK?"

It had been only a little more than a week since all hell broke loose in Alaska. The last frontier. Yeah, that's right. Gavin was as friendly as ever and seemed eager to see what she walked away with. He was surprised that it only took her three days to complete the interview, but dismissed it quickly, assuming Marren was as professional as they come.

She had finished the article and re-read it at least a hundred times, even neglecting sleep to do so. This was her career on the line after all, and she wanted it to be perfect. It had been the most difficult slab of time in her life. Funny, but true. It was actually a lot more difficult than the four months she had spent in the hospital three years ago. It was just a broken heart, but evidently a broken heart needs much more energy to heal than a broken body.

It was even more laughable that this broken heart was caused by a man that she had known for all of three days. Three measly days. But over the course of her mending she realized that although she only knew him physically for three days, she loved him for three years, give or take.

Gavin was on the phone being as personable and pleasant as one could be and, amazingly enough, not faking it. He looked over at Marren and raised his finger to tell her that he would only be one more minute as she nervously clutched the bag containing the finished article. Finally he hung up the telephone after making a lunch date and smiled at her as he took a deep breath.

"OK, Miss Lang," he started, rubbing his hands together as if he were settling in for his favorite meal. "What have you got for me?"

Her heart was thumping in a very un-Marrenlike fashion as she opened the flap of her bag. Reaching inside, she grasped the handful of papers – her finished draft – and handed it over his desk to him. He took the stack and leaned back in his chair. He was quiet for a moment and then his eyes grew wide with surprise and shock. He glanced up at her and then back to the draft, reading on. "Is this true?" he asked. Marren nodded. After twenty grueling minutes, Gavin finished the last page and looked up at her. The expression on his face was of complete disbelief. "This is beautiful," he said. "This is a masterpiece. I can't believe it . . ."

Ed had been a Godsend. If he hadn't shown up when he did, Shane would surely have drunk himself to death, blaming it on a broken heart . . . that was clear in his poetry. It took him six full days to recuperate from that drunk. A lot of puking, so much so that his back ached from the heaves, a lot of sweats and a lot of soul searching. Christ, you'd think he was a fuckin' heroine addict the way he was knocked on his ass from it.

Ed had counted fourteen empty "truth serum" bottles, and sixteen empty beer bottles. It was a miracle, as he put it, that Shane could even find enough hours in the day to drink as much as he did. "I wouldn't want to be your liver right now," he said as he cleaned up.

Marren. He missed her and had let go of the anger. The supposed interview would be out in another few months and he had accepted the fact that the shit was going to hit the fan. Within his acceptance and sobriety, there was an insight that he couldn't ignore. All he wanted was to be left alone and that was exactly how it was going to turn out. As soon as everyone found out that he had shafted them and lied to them, they would blackball him. It only made sense. They would detest him and deface him and after all the hubbub died down, he really would be left alone. He only hoped that Marren had cared enough about him, or at least respected him enough, not to lead them directly to his door.

July brought warmer weather and twenty-one hours of

daylight, the sun only setting fully at 12:37AM the morning of the first and rising at ten after three AM. The temperature topped out to a sweltering average of sixty-eight degrees although some would argue that they had read their thermometers at well over seventy in the sun. The ice and snow capped mountains remained as a reminder, however, that another cold winter would soon be upon them. Summer never touched the tops of the mountains, or not visibly anyway. Shane himself didn't know. He had never been up there, but assumed that it was a much more pleasant climate down where he was. Unless, or course, you liked that kind of thing. Roughing it. Freezing your balls off.

Sometimes he missed the heat of the Oklahoma summers, but the peacefulness and beauty of Alaska would quickly toss that feeling out the window. He was happy here and knew that this was where he wanted to stay, no matter what happened. The three days he had with Marren in the house certainly warmed everything up for him. While she was there, she had given the house a life that, to him, wasn't comparable to anything. She was beautiful alright, and he thought about her every waking moment. What was she doing? Was she thinking about him? Probably not, or at least not in the way he was thinking about her. Ed had told him that she was crying on the trip into Anchorage and had admitted that she was hurting, but Shane was so self absorbed in his own pain, he didn't take it in . . .

That first Saturday after she left, Shane had stumbled into the washroom to shower, like Ed had told him to do. The hot water only dizzied him more than he already was and he decreased its flow, opting for a cooler temperature. The feeling of the water pouring over his head and body seemed to awaken a part of him that had passed out days before with the drunk. A strength of sorts. While it was true that finding her story disappointed him like he had never been disappointed before, it also let him remember what it was he had wanted to get away from in the first place. The anger he felt toward her that day had dissolved and shaped itself into something softer. Pity maybe? For himself? Yes, a little, but he was only human. Mostly, it was pity for her. He had higher hopes of how the entire plan would work out. He had thought he saw something in her eyes the night of the accident, and in her writing, that had lifted his heart. Lifted it indeed. It only brought it up to a place that would make it more painful for him when it came crashing down and shattered into a zillion jagged and cutting bits. He pitied her for being sucked in by the illusion of what success could do for her.

He wandered back out of the washroom and into his room to get into some clean clothes. There still were no sheets on the bed and her empty pack of cigarettes remained on the bedside table. An ashtray had four butts in it, one of which had the slight tint of a natural looking lipstick on the filter. He stomach tightened and he quickly clothed himself and left the room. His walking was not as stumbling as it had been an hour before, but his movements felt as if they belonged to someone else. The drunk had taken over every inch of him, inside and out. The alcohol flowed through his veins and had leaked into his soul. Ed was right. It was a miracle he was still alive. Surely he had poisoned himself severely.

Ed had made him some eggs and toast and put on a pot of strong coffee. The coffee was good, but the food didn't interest Shane in the least. It didn't turn his guts (that would happen all on its own, later) but it didn't strike him as a necessity. Ed pulled up a chair across the table from him and sat down, lighting a cigarette.

"Ya gonna eat that or ya just gonna stare at it?"

"I'm not too hungry, Ed."

"Christ, Shane . . . she's just a woman," Ed sighed.

"That she is. That she certainly is," Shane replied.

"So she fucked ya over. Shane, buddy, she isn't the only woman on the planet. Hell, we have quite a few real love-lies up Anchorage way. You put on that charm of yours and they'll trip over each other to get to ya."

"Ed," Shane started, beginning to feel like he would like another drink and then a moment later feeling a stronger need for sleep, " . . . it ain't that I need a woman. It ain't that I need to get laid . . ."

"I know, I know . . . you love her. Well, it's an ugly fact of life that sometimes they don't love ya back, man. At least not as hard," Ed said.

"I just need to let go of the disappointment is all," Shane said, attempting to eat. "I guess I just expected too much from her."

"Are ya going to submit those poems you got out there?"

Shane shook his head slowly, finding the world was not keeping up and looking as if petroleum jelly were smeared across it. "I don't even know what I was writing."

Ed stared at him for a few moments, then looked down at his watch. "Do ya need me to stay a while?"

"No. I'm fine."

Ed got up and went to the cupboard under the sink. He pulled the few remaining bottles of 'Juice' out and placed them in a paper bag. "Sorry Shane. I can't leave these with you until ya get your sanity back. That quarter bottle out in the living room'll see ya through the hangover, so make it last. I'll check in on ya next week."

Shane wanted to get up and take the bag away from him but simply didn't have the energy in him to even argue. Ed left the room and then the house. Shane could hear the plane's engine start up and then heard it take off. He lit a cigarette, pushing the plate in front of him away, and placed his head in his hands. With his eyes shut, the world spun. He didn't even bother smoking the cigarette, but put it out in the eggs and got up. He made his way out to the sofa and laid down. He slept for six hours before the thick nausea woke him and caused him to rush to the bathroom to throw up. It seemed never ending, his body wanting nothing to do with itself and trying to evict his insides from its shell.

He woke on the bathroom floor three hours later feeling like he had been hit repeatedly with a two by four. He would be blessed with the dry heaves four more times over the next two days and then attempt to eat just to have something to throw up. It took a total of four days to start feeling somewhat normal again and another day just to be able to hold food down. He refrained from touching the 'Juice' until that last day. He knew it would probably help him at least keep his food in, but the smell of it revolted him. When he was finally able to hang on to some food, he took a belt of the Juice and then another and dammit if it didn't make him feel a whole lot better.

He capped the bottle and then made his way over to the desk by the window, gathering up the mass of poetry that he had written. He stepped out on to the front porch, sat down and began to read.

Marren had picked up some groceries and a bottle of wine on her way home from Gavin's office. Was there something to celebrate? There should be. Gavin loved it. He couldn't believe it. She didn't feel like celebrating, however. She felt a cold and lonely ache in her middle. She made herself dinner but only took a few bites of it before bringing it back to the kitchen and leaving it on the counter. She retreated back out to her living room to sit by the candlelight with her wine. Her mind was filled with Shane, as was her heart. Not wanting him in either place, she closed her eyes but was unable to stop the memory of his kisses. His hands. His embrace. The way he smelled. His eyes. Him and everything he was.

Without warning, tears overflowed from her eyes. She realized that she really had fallen in love with him and wished that if there was a God, he would have clued her in on this fact before she started filling in that second notebook. She could still be there right now, if she hadn't. Laughing with him as they interviewed the old man. Going for walks. Sitting by the fire. Making love. God dammit!

She had thought of writing him a letter and somehow getting it to Ed Lawry so he could deliver it to Shane for her, but the look in Shane's eyes when he found the notebook . . . it was of betrayal. It was of thick hurt and discouragement. No. It was better just to leave it be.

Back before she had even accepted the assignment, Gavin had given her a copy of Shane's book, *Ugly People*. It was so she could familiarize herself with his writing. She had read some of his pieces in the past and had read the book before she agreed to take the job but at the time it was just lovely poetry. As she sat cross-legged on the couch, slightly rocking herself, her eyes found the book over on the shelf. She got up and crossed the room, picking it up. There was no picture of him on it . . . shame. Returning back to the sofa, she sat down, poured herself another glass of wine, lit a cigarette and opened the book . . .

'while I was the one dying, and that street
was good enough a church
as any cathedral . . .
but it was my hands,
stained crimson and shaking,
and it was my SELF . . .'

It was clear now. The woman, and the love that he wrote about . . . it was her. The blood that made it into so many of the poems was hers. Could feelings so strong that they would cause a man to spill his soul out the way he had on these pages, really just disintegrate? It was true that she had done him wrong, but could her actions really have destroyed what he felt for her? The way he admitted everything. The way he planned to get her up there to Alaska, false pretenses or not. The way he was the guardian angel that saved her life. The way he had made love to her . . . God, the way he had made love to her. The last time she had read this book, this beautiful book, she envisioned a horrid old man, drooling and slopping his disgusting hands about himself. Now she saw the truth. She saw Shane and her heart ached like it was being brutally ripped from her body while it still beat.

'. . . licked greedy at your wounds,'

It was three AM. The wine was gone. She wished she had bought herself another bottle. Lying down on the couch, she held the book to her chest, hugging it as she fell asleep. Dreams of Shane's smile graced her, and then the look on his face when he realized her intentions, cursed her.

They were good. Shane knew it. These pieces would show him the big green dollar signs floating in his agent's eyes. He didn't even remember writing half of them, and reading them now was like catching a whiff of sour milk. The rantings of a man appreciative of his proper drunk, his respectable drunk, letting all the pain, anger and loss lie moist and squirming on the pages . . .

'why are you listening to 'come on eileen'
in full blast and giggling
real school girl like
while dreaming of red hair, and rubbing your eyes –
'come on eileen'
why?
Why?
You rotten fucker you don't even care
just put down beer
one, 2, next,
keep going,
7 down and it's still early, and you're all alone and it seems
like an entire fucken party, you can play all the characters,
you get all the main lines and as long as this song is on
repeat you'll keep laughin' and squeelin' and it's all loud
and none cares if you cut a hole in the wall, make eyes,
drop lines, buy drinks and get in

for the long
plaster ride
saying fuck modern love
and its ridiculous orbit,
lets just hear it again, and no,
I'm not lonely, no I'm not wishin' you were here, no, no
no, shit,
baby, what
you think I'm candycanes and smilin' faces and that there's
a delivery of brown eyes that look just for me? No
I'm old man, under bridge, the old
songs, the unstable smile –

'you mean everything'

We're goin on two hrs now and it's the same story,

you've heard this enough times over
to puke, piss and shit heartache and I really
could care less – cynical, I'm getting there; certifiable,
stamped since august
of 66;
and lost,
show me one person who isn't.'

He stood up and returned inside the house, sticking the one hundred and fifty some odd pages into a drawer and closing it. He still felt weakened from the last few days of withdrawal, but made his way out to the back to chop some wood. It was time to let it go. He had allowed himself to sink into his own self-pity and pain for long enough and now it was time to get back into life. He needed wood as his stockpile had dwindled. After restocking himself, he would drive into town and get a few supplies and groceries, maybe even a bottle of something to get him back up to his fighting weight. Food still wasn't something he was terribly taken by but he knew that by forcing himself and after a few days, he would be back to his normal self. He would also have to get out fishing and hunting. The few days with Marren cleaned out his freezer.

There was nowhere in town that would carry anything even remotely like 'Literary Today'. On the odd occasion when some magazines and periodicals would find there way into town, they were fishing magazines, hunting magazines, and sometimes old Joe would have a couple copies of 'Playboy' stashed under the counter, but that was it.

After loading up his truck, he made his way back inside the small grocery to use the phone. He called Ed, but only got his machine . . .

"Ed. Shane here. I'm wonderin' if ya could do me a favor. For the next few months could ya grab me a copy of 'Literary Today' and fly 'em out here when ya get a chance. No rush though. I'm screwed no matter how fast I find out that I've bent over to take it. Thanks." Just as he was about to hang up the telephone, he quickly brought the receiver back up. "Oh, and you can bring back the 'Juice'. I got my sanity back, as you so eloquently put it, you sonuvva bitch. Talk to ya later."

As he drove back, he wondered if Marren had snuck a camera in and maybe taken a picture of him at some point. It wouldn't surprise him if he opened up the magazine and saw his likeness staring back at himself. It was possible that she had, but then again, it was possible that he was just paranoid. And paranoid of what? Being found out? That was a given, now. Who cares if there's a photo or not.

There was another truck parked alongside of his house as he pulled up. He recognized it as George Meek's. George ran a little bar up Dillingham way that Shane used to regular with Ed, but that novelty soon wore off. The drinks were inexpensive and pure. Nothing watered down there. But all of that was before Shane became used to his solitude. In the beginning, it got to him a little and he would drive into town a couple of times a week, meet Ed and they would get themselves pissed drunk at George's place. The establishment didn't have a name and the locals just called it "George's".

There was no one around the back of his house, so rather than enter there, he grabbed one of the boxes out of the crib of his truck and made his way around front. He couldn't imagine what business George would have with him. Could it be that on one of his drunken evenings out he forgot to pay his tab?

As he came around the corner, he saw George's eighteen-year-old daughter Myra come down from the stoop carrying a large cast iron pot. Myra Meek was the product of George and his Athabaskan wife, Leighla . . . and a lovely product she was. She had her mother's Native American complexion and bone structure, but she had George's large snow blue eyes. Shane gave her a warm but curious smile of welcome.

"Myra. What can I do for ya?"

"Shane. Ed was by last week. Said you weren't feeling very well. So I brought you up a pot of my mother's stew," she said. "It'll heal you."

Shane's smile grew more knowing. "Well, thanks. That's real kind of you and your mother."

"How are you feeling?" she asked as he reached her.

"I'm fine. A lot better, thanks. Wanna come in?"

She nodded and followed him up the steps.

Myra had a slight crush on Shane ever since he first showed his face in her father's bar. Actually, it wasn't that slight. She told all of her friends that she wanted to bear his child. "Our baby will have beautiful golden hair, just like him. And his smile, too," she had said. Her friends thought she was crazy, telling her that he was, first of all, too old for her, and secondly, he was not one of them . . . not one of Den'a, meaning not one of *the people*. She didn't care. Her father was a white man as well and he was a wonderful man of substance, just like Shane Helnsley. She had overheard Ed talking to her father when he was up a few days earlier. He had said that Shane was "hurt pretty badly and sick as a dog".

"Does he need a doctor?" Myra asked, getting in on the conversation.

"No . . . he'll be alright. Just went on a bit of a bender is all," Ed told her.

She inquired a little more into his ailment, and decided that she would give him a few days to get through it before she would drive out and offer her assistance to him.

So, now, here she was, in his house. She had never been in his house before and the first thing that came to her mind as she stepped inside was that yes . . . she would love to live here. All she had to do was make him fall in love with her, give her a child and marry her. Sounded easy enough. What man didn't want her? Yes, this place would do nicely.

"Can I get you a cup of tea or coffee?" he asked.

"Yes, please," Myra said, looking around.

Shane turned and looked at her before entering the kitchen. "Well, which one? Tea or coffee?" he asked, smiling.

"Whatever you're going to have," she smiled back. "I like your home."

Shane put the box down on the table, then gestured to her to bring him the heavy pot she was carrying. She entered the kitchen herself, and once he had relieved her of her gift, he pulled a chair out for her. "Sit down," he said.

"Do you have a cigarette?" she asked.

Shane turned from the percolator and looked down at her. "You shouldn't be smoking. Cigarettes will kill ya," he said.

"I know," she smiled. "Do you have one?"

Shane passed her his pack and his lighter, again smiling. "Don't tell your father I gave ya one. He'd string me up."

"You can put that stew in your refrigerator if you don't want any now. It heats up better."

"Thanks again," Shane said, following her instructions. "And thank your mother for me too."

"I lied," she said. "It's my mother's recipe, but *I* made it special for you."

It wouldn't be much longer that Marren would have to do this. Going out to these damn clubs and listening to bands that she didn't particularly like. Her days at 'Room' were numbered now, or at least that was the idea. Tonight she had to actually hang around after the show and interview the band. What was it they called themselves again? 'Gin Ninety-three'. What the hell did that mean? Didn't matter. Just another night. Just another band. Another job.

The music pounded, reverberating in her chest and feeling almost choking. She ordered herself a whiskey straight up and sat down at the bar waiting for 'Gin Ninety-three' to take the stage. The deafening music from the sound system flowed around her and the smell of clove cigarettes engulfed her. Neither dulled her thoughts though. She could have had every one of her senses overtaken and overwhelmed and she still would not have been able to keep Shane off her mind. She remembered how quiet it was up there in Alaska. She recalled the night he made her listen as hard as she could to pick up on the sounds he could hear. The wind. The water. The crickets, and yes, the raccoons getting their dinner out of his trash cans. She smiled at the memory and reached back, touching the scar on the back of her head where it had been split open. He had been there and she thought he was an angel that had come down to take her away to some better place.

"Hey. Hi," a voice said, waking her.

She looked up to see a young man standing next to her with a beer in his hand. Nice looking. Long dark hair and a face that definitely had a long trail of broken hearts behind it. "Do I know you?" she asked.

"Zach Hyde. Gin Ninety-three," he said. "You're Marren Lang, right?"

"Yes," she said.

"Guess you're interviewing us later."

"Mmmm hmmm," she confirmed into her drink.

"Mind if I sit down here?" he asked.

Marren shook her head and watched him as he hoisted himself up onto the stool next to her. "You're not going to try and buy my kind words are ya?" she smiled.

"You aren't selling are ya?" he smiled back.

Marren chuckled and shook her head. "No. No I'm not. What are you selling?"

"Nothin'. I'm buyin'," Zach said.

"You're buyin'," she repeated with a slight tint of sarcasm that he apparently didn't catch. "OK, what are you buyin'?"

"Your next drink," he said.

Myra's company was a breath of fresh air. Her laughter in the house seemed a blessing and lifted Shane's spirit some. She had heated up her stew for him and served him as well as having some herself. Shane asked if she wanted to have a bit of whiskey with him and she did. It was brand name whiskey that he had bought while in town, and tasted quite watery to him compared to Ed's Juice, but it would have to do for now. He told Myra again not to let on to her father that he was contributing to the corruption of a minor, and she laughed again. As evening fell, he had not noticed that the level of the bottle had gone down to half. He looked down at his watch. 10PM. Christ, was it that late?

"It's getting late, Myra. Maybe you better get back before all the light is gone. It's a real bitch to get outta here after dark."

She peered over at him as he sat on the porch step next to her. Certainly there had to be a way to preoccupy him until the sun had completely set. There had to be some way that she could strand herself there for the night. "It's not that late," she argued.

Shane looked out at the horizon. "There's only about another hour of good light left."

Just then, Myra leaned over and kissed him. Not simply on the cheek as a thank you or anything, but right on the lips, and there was a very clear element of seduction behind it. He was surprised, but after a few moments he closed his eyes and let her. She tasted nice. His mind reeled and he felt ashamed for liking the way she felt. He put his arm around her small frame and opened his mouth as she did. Their tongues met and caressed softly as passion grew between them. A few seconds later, Shane pulled away.

"Myra. I don't think this is a good idea," he said.

She stared into his eyes with her own, clear and icy blue. "Why not? Don't you think I'm pretty?"

"Yeah, I think you're pretty," he said. "But you're eighteen and I'm . . ."

"I don't care how old you are," she said. "And I'm not a kid," she told him while she undid the buttons of her shirt and displayed herself to him.

Shane peered down at her. She really was quite beautiful and he wondered if he shouldn't just take her. Who would it hurt? Marren sure as hell wouldn't care. Before he could sort through all the thoughts and questions in his head, she kissed him again while taking his hand and placing it on her left breast. After another second, Shane picked her up and carried her into the house, straight to his bedroom. He lay her down on the still unmade bed and put his weight down on her. She slowly began to undress him as he did the same to her, but then he stopped and sat up.

"I'm sorry. I can't do this," he said.

"Yes you can," she whispered, behind his back.

She reached over and took his arm, trying to urge him to lie down again, but he stood up. "Look, Myra . . . thank you for dinner and thank you for . . . I just . . . I can't do this to you," he said.

The look of hurt on her face was almost unbearable and he had to look away. "Is it something about me that you don't like?" she asked.

"No," Shane mumbled, putting his shirt back on. "You're beautiful."

"Then why?" Myra begged, her voice trembling with the threat of tears.

Shane looked over at her on his unmade bed. "You're a wonderful girl, Myra. But I'm in love with another. I can't give you what I've already given away."

She thought of telling him that all she wanted from him was a child, but then thought again. His child. What would that child be without him? It was him that she wanted. The piece of him that she wanted would only torment her if she couldn't have him as well. "I'm sorry," she whimpered, putting her clothes back on.

"I'll drive you out to the road," he said.

Marren led Zach up the stairs to her apartment after having enjoyed his company at the club. He was charming and witty, not to mention attractive. Gin Ninety-three was relatively entertaining. Energetic. They sounded like a lot of other bands, however, as was the way with the music scene these days. If something worked, everyone did it. Zach was the drummer, and a very good one; probably the best part of the band. The interview went well but felt uncomfortable because she knew that he had set his sights on her and she seemed to be headed toward willingness. They had a wonderful time together, and as the evening wore on the jokes and laughter had started to become touchy feely and it was very clear what he had in mind.

He had brought a bottle scotch with him, and once inside her place asked her for a couple of glasses. As she went to get them, Zach sat down on the sofa and picked up the book that sat on the coffee table.

"*Ugly People*. What's this about?" he called to her in the kitchen.

She came back out with the glasses, eyeing him as he eyed the book. "Poetry," she said.

"Oh yeah? You like poetry?"

"Some," she said.

He opened the cover and quickly skimmed over the first piece. "Wow, this guy is pretty fucked up, isn't he?"

"So it seems," she said, placing the glasses down on the table and heading over to the stereo.

Zach read a few more of the pieces, laughing at most. "Wow, this stuff is twisted. This is great!" Marren returned to the sofa after putting some music on and snatched the book out of his hands. She slapped it shut and tossed it back on the table. Zach gazed at her dumbfounded. "What's the matter? You don't like that book or something?"

"I like it fine, but I'd rather not hover over it all night."

Zach smiled, taking her statement to mean that she was more interested in other activities. He poured some scotch into the glasses as she sat down next to him but kept her distance. "Why don't ya sit a little closer? I don't bite," he said, offering her her glass.

Marren smiled, beginning to question herself for bringing him back to her place at all. She wasn't on the market for a relationship and certainly wasn't the one night stand type. Was this just some attempt to get Shane out of her head? And if so, would it work? She moved over a foot or so and accepted the glass from him. "Cheers," she muttered under her breath, downing it.

"Well, I guess you aren't trying to get *me* drunk," he laughed.

He moved closer to her still and began kissing her neck.

Marren wanted to pull away from him but didn't. She poured herself another drink while he continued to kiss her, moving up her neck to her ear. His breath felt good. Warm. She sipped at her drink, refusing to close her eyes because she knew that Shane would be waiting for her right there behind her lids. This was Zach Hyde . . . not Shane. "You act like you do this a lot," she smirked.

Zach stopped kissing her and peered into her eyes. "Well, you don't seem to be fightin' me," he smiled. "It's not like this is a hobby of mine or anything. I find you to be a real gorgeous lady and you turn me on. Is that OK?"

"Yeah. That's fine," she smiled, wanting her thoughts and memories to leave her alone. Silently begging them to.

Zach leaned in and kissed her softly on the lips. A moment later he put his arms around her, pulling her closer to him, and began kissing her passionately. She let him. There was no sense fighting him or saying no. He was good looking, and contrary to her first impression of him he wasn't some air headed idiot. Why not give him a whirl. Maybe in time he could knock the poet out of her head and heart all together. Zach pushed her back and began fumbling with her clothes. She was about to start helping him, but her stomach turned on her. This was wrong. This was so fucking wrong. She loved Shane and just wasn't open to let this happen. She didn't want anyone else's hands on her except Shane's. She put her hands on his chest and stopped him. "I can't do this," she said.

"No? How come?" he asked.

"It doesn't matter. Just . . . could you get off of me, please?"

Zach sat up. "More time? That's cool. I can wait," he said.

"No. Don't," she came back. Zach looked over at her, his dark eyes questioning her and she tried to explain. "I'd be using you to forget someone else."

"So use me," he said. "Maybe it'll work," he added, trying to smile.

She appreciated his charm. "I wish it would . . . but I know it won't."

CHAPTER 9

Myra was quiet in the passenger seat as Shane drove her father's truck through the near darkness. He felt horrible for having to turn her down. If things were different he wouldn't have. He would have had sex with her. Myra really was a wonderful girl and one that he would have gladly pursued a relationship with, but there were some things that simply wouldn't allow it. First, she was so incredibly young. If he wasn't mistaken, she had only just turned eighteen the month before. And secondly, he couldn't allow himself to hurt her by loving someone else. It just wouldn't be fair to her to make love to her and wish it was Marren.

Once he reached the road, he stopped the truck and looked over at her. "I'm sorry Myra."

"It's OK," she mumbled, half-heartedly.

He grabbed his rifle and climbed out of the truck. "You be careful driving back," he told her.

"I will," she assured, sliding over the seat and taking her place behind the wheel.

Shane closed the door and leaned on the window for a moment. "You understand, don't ya?"

"Oh yeah . . . I understand," she said, some bitterness coming through with her tone.

"Hey," Shane said, taking her chin in his fingers and gently forcing her to look at him. "C'mon. Don't just dump me cos I can't . . ."

"You dumped me," she interrupted. "Shane . . ."

"I didn't dump you, Myra. I'm always here and you can come around whenever ya want. I like you. I'm just tryin' to do what's right. I'm still your friend."

141

She glared at him. "You know, every man wants me. You're the one that can have me. You can have all of me. You can just take me."

Shane took in a deep breath and looked out into the darkness. "No Myra, I can't take you," he said.

"Someday you're going to want me," she said, stepping on the gas and squealing away.

Shane had to back away from the truck so she wouldn't run over his feet with her back tire. He watched her taillights until they turned around the first bend in the road and disappeared. He turned quietly, and started his twenty-minute walk back to the house.

He knew the land well and didn't need a flashlight – the sky's glow and light of the moon would guide him. Since living out here, his hearing and eyesight had strengthened and he felt at ease being out at night. He would be able to hear if anything was nearby and after a quick adjustment he would be able to see it well enough to protect himself. He wasn't worried.

As he walked, his pace even and his steps light, he thought about Myra and the way she must be feeling. Her pride was probably suffering badly. When she had kissed him he wanted her, and he cursed himself for not being able to get past what his heart was telling him. Still, what it was telling him was a truth he couldn't deny. He loved Marren and it was going to take a while to get over her. He knew that in the past, after the accident, he had tried bedding some of his students in an attempt to forget the angel he had seen, but it didn't work. It didn't work then and it wouldn't work now. Especially now. It wasn't just an idea any longer. He had met her, come to know her, and he had made love to her. The love he already felt for her only flowered into a harsh reality. He really loved her. Yes, it was going to take quite some time before his entire being didn't ache for her the way he was aching for her now. A hunger that couldn't be fed, it was near agonizing. Maybe in time he could release the need he felt for Marren and move on. Maybe in time he could find something with Myra, but not now.

Zach left without argument and took his scotch with him. *'Figures'*, she thought. She had been hoping that he would leave without it, maybe forgetting it, or just not caring, but no such luck. Then another thought passed through her mind. Maybe she shouldn't have acted the way she did. Maybe she had just made a mistake . . .

No. She had not made a mistake. When she had closed her eyes for an instant during Zach's kiss, all she could see was Shane. But those weren't Shane's lips. Zach kissed nice, but Shane had these lips on him that could make the earth move. Now, she sat alone in her apartment, wanting a drink. It was late and she didn't much like having to go out, but damn if she didn't honestly need that drink. She grabbed her car keys and headed out.

It was easily still eighty-five degrees outside and she could feel the humidity swallow her and cause her shirt to immediately stick to her skin. As she drove she realized that she had passed the store she meant to stop at. She didn't turn around, however. She kept driving. After a ways, she turned onto 21st. She knew exactly where she was going but wasn't certain why. Maybe an answer would come to her when she reached her destination. Something to tell her that she had made the right choice about Shane. Something to justify her actions.

One block from Washington, she pulled over in front of a small store. It was the same store she had gone into the night her bastard ex, David, hit her with his car and almost killed her. She got out of the car and looked down at the road. She didn't know exactly where she had landed on the street, but it was very near where she was standing now. And he had been here. Shane. If he hadn't have been here, there was a very good chance that she wouldn't be standing here today. Funny thing was, standing here today almost didn't seem worth it anymore. In the little while that she had spent with him, he made her feel things that she didn't know existed. These feelings were huge and warm. They excited her. He excited her. The memory of time they spent together came from all directions and surrounded her. One moment she found herself smiling and remembering fondly, and the next she would experience a crushing pain like she'd never known. She crossed her arms, holding onto each, and let a shiver take her even in the heat of the evening. She missed him so badly. She knew it now . . . she really loved him, and without him everything just seemed kind of dead.

Before she knew it, the sun was rising. She had left her apartment to go get herself a bottle of something at around three AM and now the sun was rising. She had been standing here for the better part of three hours. Was she losing her mind? It certainly looked that way, but she felt a connection with him here. God, she wanted to get herself to the airport and fly back to Alaska . . . right fucking now. Just go to Alaska and then hire someone to fly her out to Shane's. She could beg his forgiveness and he would forgive her. Yes, he would forgive her and then he would hold her and never let her go.

Instead, she drove herself home and slept that Sunday morning away.

The monitor screen buzzed and glowed. Since being in Alaska, he had never once hooked up his computer. The stack of poetry lay next to his keyboard waiting to be typed and he sat back and stared at it for a moment.

144

The sound of Ed's Cessna zooming overhead broke the silence in the room and Shane peered out the window to see him coming in for a landing. He lifted himself out of his chair and headed out to meet him. Ed got out of the Skylane pulling a box out with him. Thank God, he brought the 'Juice'. Whiskey was fine, but it didn't have the personality Ed's Juice did. Needless to say, a personality that rich could never be absent in his house without being missed. It was the way the astronauts probably felt without their *Tang*. It was like the proverbial "day without sunshine". Sad, but true.

Shane strolled out toward the plane to greet him. "Ed."

"You're looking well, Shane," Ed greeted back, bracing the box with his knee and sticking his hand out to shake.

"Can ya come in for a drink?" Shane asked, shaking his hand.

"Sure. Sure. There's another box if you want to grab it," Ed said.

Shane opened the passenger side door and pulled out the second box, seeing that three copies of 'Literary Today' sat on top of the twelve bottles of 'Juice'. His heart began to pound even though he knew without a doubt that it was still too early to see anything. The two men walked back to the house, Shane stepping inside first. Immediately he pulled a bottle out and opened it. "Thanks," he said, tipping it up and appearing to feel great relief as it flowed through his veins again.

He passed the bottle to Ed and then walked across the room to the shelf in the corner. He pulled out a box from behind a row of books and counted out one hundred and twenty dollars. Replacing the box, he crossed the room again and offered Ed the money.

"One case is on me," he said, counting out sixty and giving it back to Shane. "I'm proud of you."

"Proud?" Shane repeated, taking the money and looking confused. "For what?"

"Not using Myra Meek to forget that writer lady."

"How did you know about that?" Shane asked, taking the bottle back and taking a swig from it, appreciating it.

"My niece Linda is a friend of Myra's. She told her all about it. Guess she didn't bargain on Linda telling her mother everything and my sister telling *me* everything."

"Jesus," Shane breathed. "I didn't know there was such a fuckin' grapevine all the way up here."

"Where there's women, there's grapevines," Ed said. "Anyway, from the sound of it I think you probably did the right thing." He looked down at the desk and the running computer with the poetry sitting next to it. "You're working," he stated, picking up one of the pages and peering down at it . . .

Finely Skinned Clouds
'Her mouth is strange
Her eyes are strange
Pan-fried sunshine
Winter recall
Laughed real fine while playing in the gutter
(embracing despair)
Floating head, cum/words drip off golden lips and
the windowpane slams on clumsy thumb . . .'

Shane nodded. "Thinkin' about it."

"Good. Good. I was wondering how far that box of money was going to take you before you ran out."

"It isn't the money," Shane said, leaning up against the desk. "Maybe Marren was right, ya know? Anyway, my little vacation is about to end. No sense in holding it back any more."

"She still on your mind?" Ed asked, sitting down in the chair and picking up the first poem from the pile.

"She'll always be on my mind."

"But she screwed you, Shane. How can you let a woman like that . . ."

"Ed, she was just doin' what she felt she had to do. For herself. I can't blame her for wantin' to up her career. She was just lookin' out for herself. And if you think about it, she really didn't know me."

"Selfish," Ed mumbled, looking back down at the page in his hand and beginning to read. "This is about her, isn't it?"

"Aren't they all?" Shane smirked as he turned to look out the window.

"Maybe Myra isn't such a bad idea after all," Ed said. Shane looked down at him, passing him the bottle, but Ed declined the offer. "I have to get back. Got a charter out to Wood River."

"Ya don't think she's too young?" Shane asked, bringing the bottle back up to his lips.

"Myra? She's eighteen," Ed replied.

"That's pretty young."

"Yeah, if you were sixty. Shane, you're what? Thirty something?"

"Three."

"If she were twenty, would she be too young for you then?"

Shane thought about his question and about what he was implying. "I dunno. And besides, I thought ya said you were proud of me."

"I did. I am," Ed said. "But that doesn't mean that I don't think you're crazy. You, my friend, must have one hell of a strong will." Shane chuckled and lit a cigarette as Ed stood up and read a little further . . .

'. . . The light doesn't sound too good
The reception ain't comin in so clear
And mental instability
is just another term for freedom.'

He shoved the poem into Shane's gut. "I can imagine what the rest of that stack is like. This is sick. Good but sick. It's very you. I think ya should send it in."

"Maybe," Shane said.

After Ed left, Shane walked into his bedroom and stared at the bed for a moment. He let his memory drift back to when Marren was lying in it. That first night that he had to carry her in and lay her down. He had wanted her so badly he could taste it. Then the night she came out and woke him. As he remembered, his heart swelled into a large thumping mass of pain. He heavily clomped over to the small storage cubbyhole of a closet he had built and pulled out some linen. He made the bed up quickly and then left the room, not letting his mind wander back to what Ed had said . . . *"Maybe Myra isn't such a bad idea after all."*

He sat back down at his desk and picked the three magazines out of the box Ed had brought. He leafed through them finding nothing, but he already knew he wouldn't. He more than likely would find it in the next issue, however. Him. Unmasked and naked for everyone to gawk at. Reaching under a stack of older papers he pulled out Marren's novel and turned it over to gaze at her photograph on the back cover. He hadn't looked at it since she left, almost feeling afraid to. Her image brought the memory of her back in such a strong wave, it gave him a lightheaded feeling. Leaning the book up against a lamp so he had a good view of it, he lit another cigarette and placed it in the ashtray next to his poetry, and began to type.

It had been just over four months since she had returned from Alaska. Her article on Shane Helnsley was to be printed in this month's issue of 'Literary Today'. It would be hitting the newsstands today as a matter of fact. Marren dressed for work deciding that she really didn't want to see the finished article, but knowing that she really should have a copy for her resume. She had already been paid for the work and it was more generous than she had originally anticipated. When the check was in her hand, the notion came to her that it was enough to see her through a year of unemployment. The amount printed out on that check caused her to think of all the things Shane had said to her about success. Was this the kind of money that he generated? Was this the kind of money that was being thrown at him? It was a perverse amount and just holding it in her hand caused her mouth to become dry and her breath to become short. In fact, this amount would easily see her through a year. A year that she could spend writing another novel. She had the story growing in her mind already. It was in there already written. Already lived. Of course she wouldn't use real names or places, but it was the story that had taken place between Shane and herself.

The idea still pestered her, but she continued to go about her routine, seemingly ignoring it. The check she had received had been deposited into her bank account but had so far gone unspent. It was as if the money itself was dirty. It felt as if she had stolen it and she really didn't want to touch it.

At the office, she was all the buzz. Everyone was talking about 'Literary Today' and dying to know how the whole thing turned out. She had been secretive about it, saying that it was just another job and wishing everyone would just leave her alone about it. He was a constant on her mind any-way, but when they would ask or mention it in any way, the crushing pain in her chest would close in around her. When it came, it came the way nervous butterflies usually would. Starting deep within her and rushing up. But this feeling wasn't butterflies. It was a sickly, heavy pain that started in her core, growing quickly and then consuming her from the inside out.

Mid morning, Wallace from a few desks down came trotting in waving the newest issue of 'Literary Today'. "Marren . . . it's out."

Her heart sank and she wanted to just run and hide. He came up beside her desk and plopped it down in front of her while a few others gathered around. An odd feeling of claustrophobia overtook her and she simply picked the magazine up and handed it back to someone. "You all go ahead and look at it. I've already seen it."

"Of course you've seen it," Wallace said. "You wrote it. But don't you want to see it in print?" He turned to another coworker that stood behind Marren. The one she had handed the magazine to. "I read it. It's amazing. It's . . ."

She couldn't stand it any longer. She pushed her chair out and took off running out of the large room trying to keep her tears at bay. A few of her coworkers called after her but she didn't stop and she didn't slow down until she was outside the building. The world outside seemed to be moving in slow motion. All the sounds of the street were muffled and seemingly smudged into the background. She half walked, half jogged to her car a block down, not noticing that the tears she was trying to keep under control had escaped and were flowing freely from her eyes. When she climbed into her car and shut the door, closing the outside sounds out, her tears were more evident to herself. The sound of her sobs choked out of her and a glance in the rear view told her that her mascara was smeared all over her cheeks.

* * * *

It was the wee hours of the morning when he finished. His fingers were slow and clumsy over the keyboard at first, being a bit rusty, but soon they remembered where everything was. Typed, there ended up being one hundred pages, holding eighty-six poems. He couldn't believe he had written that many during his drunk and was even more amazed that each one was fresh. One would think that stagnancy would settle in after several pieces with the same subject matter, but that was not the case here. Although all hovered around the same subject, none rivaled the other. Each one had another facet of feeling to examine. Another corner of hurt to inflict or struggle through. There was bitterness and resentment that came in every color imaginable. Anger in a crimson that burned the eyes straight through to the soul.

He clicked the computer off and made his way to the bedroom, peeling his shirt off over his head on his way. Sitting down on the edge of the bed, he pulled his boots off and then his jeans. He crawled under the covers then lay there, staring up into the darkness. Things were becoming clearer to him, maybe through the poetry, maybe over the time that helps heal, but the steps before him were unequivocal. Life as he knew it over the past three years was going to change and he was going to have to change with it. There wasn't going to be a riot or anything like that, but there would be the knowledge. It simply wouldn't be or even feel the same any longer. The sense of complete isolation and solitude would be gone. Hell, it already was gone. It was gone the moment he read what Marren had written.

That morning it happened, the first thing that crossed his mind was to rip the pages out of her notebook and burn them in the fireplace, but what good would that have done? It was in her head anyway. She could just write it all back down.

If that was the way she felt, and that was what she felt she had to do, then that was what she was going to do. There was nothing he could have done to stop it. What was still burning him, however, was the fact that she gave herself to him and obviously asked for him in return. What kind of person would do that? Heartless? Cold? How could she have felt the way she did about him and then fall into bed with him? How could she have shown him as much passion as she had and accept his if she thought him selfish and miserly? It made him smile slightly, but he felt as if he had been violated.

Sleep wasn't going to come easy, the noisy head syndrome being in full force and making him restless. He also felt extremely *uncomfortable* in his comfortable bed. He hadn't slept in it since she left, opting to pass out on the couch every night instead. After a couple of hours tossing and turning, he finally fell asleep, but couldn't even find relief there. She filled his dreams. Her beautiful body. Soft. Velvet. Warm. Poetry in his arms.

She stopped at the store on her way home to pick up a few things, and grabbed a bottle of whiskey for herself. She now had a taste for the stuff, although nothing was quite like Ed's Juice. Everything tasted so faded and one dimensional in comparison. Once home, she stepped into her apartment building to hear her phone ringing up the first flight of stairs. Normally she wouldn't care and she would let the machine pick it up for her, but for reasons she didn't want to admit to herself, she ran to get up the stairs. Fumbling with her keys, she finally got in and grabbed the phone on the fourth ring hoping as hard as she could that it was him. If she wanted it to be Shane hard enough, maybe it would be. It wasn't. It was a telephone solicitor trying to sell her a carpet cleaning service.

"I don't have any carpets," she said.

"We do upholstery as well, Ma'am. And we have a special on . . ."

"I don't have any furniture either," Marren said, starting to hang up the phone.

"Well, what do you sit on?" the disembodied voice asked.

Marren brought the phone back up to her ear for a moment. "My ass. What do *you* sit on?"

She sat down on the couch and began to laugh at what she had just said to the poor soul on the other end of the phone. Just doing their job was all and she had been so rude. It was funny, but her laughter was from frustration and, she knew, her mind's attempt to release the pressure inside of herself. It was then that the nervous laughter turned back into tears of complete and utter unhappiness. What the hell was going on here? Why was all of this taking such a toll on her? She was going to have to let this go. She certainly couldn't go on this way, and if it got any worse she thought she was going to lose her mind. That was just it though. It *was* getting worse, and the article coming out only caused it to be amplified about a hundred times.

She composed herself as best she could with a sigh and a hand roughly wiping the tears from her cheeks. She went to the kitchen and got herself a glass, then returned to the sofa, opened the bottle and poured herself some. Just then, the intercom by the door buzzed and scared the life out of her. Who the hell would be calling on her at this time? It was just before the lunch hour and she decided that it was probably someone wanting to sell her something else. Probably some form of religion. Pamphlets and smiles. She sighed and made her way over, pressing the button when she got there.

"Yes?" she asked.

"Marren? It's Gavin."

What the hell? What could he want? "C'mon in. First door on your right, on the first landing."

She buzzed him in and a few moments later she opened the door for him. He looked down at the drink in her hand and then at his watch, smiling. "Holy cow. Power brunch?"

"Mmmm, yes," she said, stepping to one side as a way of inviting him in.

He peered into her face, noticing the puffy red eyes and the shadow of mascara that had been wiped away. "Marren, is everything OK? I called you at work, but they said you weren't there."

"Yes, everything is fine," she said.

"Are you sick? You look like you've been crying."

"Um . . . soap opera. I'm a real sucker for those things," she lied.

"Well . . ." Gavin said, clapping his hands together. "Did you see it? I brought you one just in case you hadn't," he said, pulling an issue of Literary Today out of his breast pocket. It flopped open as soon as he did and he handed it to her. "Not only do I think you deserve a perversely expensive lunch to celebrate, but I have a job offer for you that I think you will be interested in."

"Job offer?" she echoed, taking the magazine and putting it down on the coffee table. Right on the cover in large gold-ish print was an index of the month's features. The first one on the list and in the biggest print read . . . "Shane Helnsley - The End of the Silence - by Marren Lang".

Her stomach turned and she looked away from it taking a good hit of whiskey.

Gavin smiled. "C'mon out to lunch and I'll tell you all about it. I have a car waiting out front."

"I . . . um . . . alright," she said, downing the rest of her drink and grabbing her bag.

* * * *

She definitely had all eyes on her as they were shown to their table. As far as she was concerned it was her choice of dress. Everyone in the place was in three piece suits, expensive business dresses and blazers. She had on a pair of jeans, a "Gin Ninety-three" T-shirt and a pair of Doc Martins. Her hair was left down and loose and was tousled and wind blown. What she didn't realize, however, was that most of the people looking at her were doing so because of the article. Everyone who was anyone knew Gavin and his choice of establishments was one where most of St. Louis' publishing community had their business luncheons.

They were seated and Gavin ordered a bottle of champagne. "Can you feel it?" he asked as the waiter walked away.

"Feel what?" she asked.

"You're a success," he said. "You're the talk of the town."

"Oh, c'mon," she laughed.

"You are. And this is just the beginning. Have you ever heard of Lionel Turnish?"

"Mmmm . . . no. I don't think so," she replied.

"He's the CEO for Zinnia Publishing. I was talking to him this morning and he wants to meet with you."

"Zinnia wants to meet with me? Why? For what?"

"Your next novel. Lionel also wants the squib on the publisher that has the rights to your first. Zinnia wants to buy it."

"This is a joke, right?" she smiled, looking up at the waiter who had brought the champagne in an ice bucket.

"No joke. I told you this would happen."

The champagne was poured and the waiter waited for Gavin to test the product. He did and said it was fine. He held his glass up to Marren. "Are you ready for one helluva ride, Miss Lang?"

She picked up her glass and clinked his, feeling at a loss for words. "No."

"No? What do you mean, no?"

Marren stared at him for a moment and then glanced around the room. She took in a deep breath and swallowed hard, looking back at Gavin. "Gavin . . . I fell in love with him."

Gavin cracked up laughing and it was so loud the people at the next table looked over at him. "Ah, you are a funny one, aren't you," he said.

She didn't laugh. She didn't even smile. The seriousness on her face was enough to strike fear in anyone's heart. "It's true," she said.

The smile on Gavin's face remained glued there but had lost all of its previous ambitions. Feeling that perhaps he had either heard her wrong or wasn't quite clear about who she was talking about, he asked, "OK, you fell in love with who?"

"Shane," she said. "I fell in love with him and I feel like I'm going to die without him. I'm losing my fucking mind, that's for sure."

He bound the stack of papers with a simple aluminum band. Most publishers and agents liked to receive works unbound, but Shane didn't give a shit. His agent would accept his work if it was scribbled on a fucking wad of toilet paper. Binding it would make it easier for him to tote around with him. He had called Ed the day before, telling him that he had to get out of there and fast. Ed would be overhead any minute to take him to Anchorage. The latest issue of 'Literary Today' sat on his desk next to his manuscript with the bold gold print on the front cover . . . *"Shane Helnsley - The End of the Silence - by Marren Lang"*. It hadn't seemed real until he read it. All the feelings he had toward it didn't hit home until he actually had it in front of him. He thought he would be able to deal with it, but the damn thing actually startled him. It shook him up and left him feeling quite different than he had anticipated.

He hadn't slept well since all of this went down. Although he didn't go on another bender, his drinking was still a little more pronounced than it had been. He couldn't get her off his mind and felt like he was indeed having a break down. What was it about this woman that always made him feel this way? And now, with the article out, it only felt magnified and more horrible than it ever had. He had to leave and save himself.

Not much was said in the plane, and after he dropped Shane off at the airport, all Shane said was, "I'll see ya."

Ed watched him as he walked away from the Skylane. He looked so out of place with all of the people around. The cement and the noise. He just didn't fit in. Ed hoped that his friend was going to be OK and wondered why he felt it was so necessary to run again. You would think the law was after him or something.

Zinnia wanted her work, just like Gavin had said. They had already sent her a publication agreement for a work that hadn't even been started yet, which had a very pleasing advance written into it. It was ludicrous. All of this because of Shane. It didn't seem right. It was late and she couldn't sleep. She sat up with a glass of whiskey and began to write, but not her new novel. She began to write a letter.

Dear Shane,
I know this letter is not welcome and may very well end up in the trash, but I never got a chance to talk to you before I left. As much as you don't think anything I

might have to say is worth listening to, I think it's worth
saying. And I need to say it.
Shane, you had told me that you loved me and I simply
cannot believe that I can't be forgiven. I know I hurt
you and I'm hoping that it makes you feel better to
know that now, you are hurting me. I'm in love with
you Shane and I've never hurt so bad in my life. I can't
stand facing the day without you. I don't want to.
Can we meet? Talk. Just talk. Please.
Marren

She included her phone number, both for work and home, and her address. She hunted down Ed Lawry's charter business on the internet and sent the letter the next morning, *Fedex* overnight. She didn't bother putting Shane's letter in a separate envelope, she just attached a small note for Ed asking him to please deliver it to Shane.

If she didn't hear back from either of them within the next two weeks, she would accept Zinnia's offer and move out to Florida to begin her new career. The move wasn't necessary but she could no longer stay where she was. Starting fresh somewhere else could only do her good. She had some friends out there that could help her with the adjustment and also help her to forget, or at least let go of the last four years.

The *Fedex* package showed up shortly before ten AM. Ed was on his way out the door when the courier arrived. He opened it in the doorway and read both the note for him and then the letter to Shane. He watched the *Fedex* truck drive away and sighed. Shane had left and, unfortunately, Ed didn't know where to get in touch with him. All he had said was that he had to get away for a while. "A good long while."

He wasn't sure of the time difference between Missouri

and Alaska, but that evening when he got in he would figure it out and then give her a call to tell her the bad news. He didn't much like the woman for what she had done to his friend. Shane was a good and honest man that wanted nothing but to be left alone to live the way he needed to. But then again, this was the woman that Shane loved, so he would do them both the favor of calling her and telling her. He knew that Shane would have wanted it that way.

Ed knew that he would be seeing Shane again, or at least, he hoped so. He was his best friend and he hurt for what the man was going through. He would have to come back sometime to pick up the rest of his things. He didn't have that much, but what he did have, Ed knew, was Shane's only world. Maybe he would be back. On the other hand, he had done this before – left everything behind and disappeared. Material objects meant nothing to Shane Helnsley. He was definitely a very curious man.

CHAPTER 10

It had been almost two weeks and Zinnia had called to set up a meeting between Marren and Lionel Turnish. Zinnia's head office was located in Jacksonville, Florida, which was only a stones throw from the locale of her new home. Most of her plans were set. She had her airline tickets to Florida, and had sold off a lot of her belongings. What hadn't been sold had been donated to the Salvation Army. All of it had been taken away the previous day. She wouldn't miss it. She had everything she needed packed up and waiting by the door. There was still another month on her lease that was paid for, but now was as good a time as any to leave. Make a clean break. The van lines would be picking up the boxes soon to deliver them to her friend's home just about thirty miles outside Jacksonville. This was it. This was the start of a new life. All she had left to do now was catch her flight, which was leaving in four hours.

She ran out to the little store down the street to get a coffee and a pack of cigarettes. She also wanted to busy herself a bit. There was nothing left that she could do with herself and sitting in an empty apartment was only depressing her more than she already was. She had sold her car for eight hundred dollars, not telling the buyer that the floor on the passenger side was little more than the carpeting, rust and cardboard. She had to walk to the store, but it was a nice September morning. Quite warm.

She took her time getting back and let her mind float to the memory of Shane. She found herself actually smiling a little at the recollection. As she walked she sipped her coffee and opened the August issue of 'Literary Today' to the page of her article. She hadn't looked at it yet, not having been able to bring herself to do it, but today she felt differently. She was saying good-bye to a part of life that meant more than any other. As difficult as that was, it was something she needed to do.

"It's good," a voice said, startling her as she approached the steps to her apartment. She looked up to see Shane sitting on the top step, holding up a copy of the magazine. He glanced down at the page his copy was folded over at and read the first line out loud . . . '*With his right hand smoothing back his sparse and matted gray hair, he clutched and fiddled with himself through his pants with his other.*' I like it."

She dropped her coffee and the styrofoam cup split as it hit the sidewalk, popping loudly and sending scalding coffee all over the pavement. "Fuck!" she breathed, looking down, but then looking back up quickly at the man sitting on the steps. "What . . . how . . . what are you doing here?"

"I have an appointment with my agent in New York," he said, waving the manuscript up for her to see. "Thought I'd stop by on my way."

"On your way to New York? Um . . . I think you took a wrong turn somewhere," she laughed. The disbelief and shock was so evident on her face and in the sound of her laugh that it almost pained him to see it.

"No. No wrong turn," he smiled, his voice low, gruff and sincere. She said nothing, just stood there with her mouth still opened from the shock of seeing him. "Why didn't you submit the truth?" he asked.

She continued to stare at him before she remembered how to speak. The answer to his question was so easy that it practically fell out of her. "Because I love you," she said.

Shane smiled and looked down at the magazine. "Ya do, huh?"

"Yes, I do."

"You're leaving here," he said as a statement.

"How do you know that?"

"The note on your mailbox to the mailman. Where ya goin?"

"Florida," Marren answered.

Shane nodded. "What's in Florida?"

"A new life. Somewhere where I could let go of everything that happened between us."

"Ah, you don't wanna let that go, Marren. Do ya?" he asked, standing up and coming down the steps to meet her at the bottom.

She looked into his eyes and melted. "Not really. But I . . . I didn't think I would ever see you again."

Shane looked down at himself, holding his hands out to his sides and then he looked back to her. "You stand corrected."

"Yes, it does appear that way, doesn't it?"

He leaned in and gave her a sweet kiss. "Jesus, I missed you," he whispered, his lips brushing hers. "Come back with me."

He caught her off guard with the kiss and her knees weakened with the touch of his lips. Then his words pulled her back. "To Alaska?" she asked, sounding surprised.

"Yeah. I don't really gotta go to New York. Just gotta hit a mailbox is all. Come back with me. Come home."

"I have to meet with Zinnia Publishing in Florida day after next," she mumbled into another of his kisses.

He pulled away from her and gazed into her eyes. "Zinnia . . . no kidding? That's great. Guess ya hit the jackpot, huh?"

"I guess," she muttered, almost feeling ashamed.

She would now get to feel success. Zinnia was probably the biggest publishing house around and they only pushed what they knew they could market. He looked deeply into her eyes. He had decided two weeks ago that he was willing to give the whole thing another shot. His writing. He wanted to do it for Marren. And now, she was being rewarded for her talent. What he felt in his heart that very moment, just looking into her eyes, told him that whether she enjoyed success or not, he wanted to be by her side through it. Maybe success wouldn't be so lonely if they had each other. "I'm glad for ya," he said.

"I'll give it up for you," she whispered.

"No ya won't. I won't let ya," he smiled.

"But, Shane . . . I want to be with you. I'd rather be with you. You're all I want," she said, her voice trembling faintly and her eyes sparkling with tears.

"I'll make ya a deal," he said. "I ain't never been to Florida. I hear it's nice. I could use a couple of days in a swanky hotel room. Run myself up a nice bill. Steal a few ashtrays. Why don't I come with ya, and then you come home with me when you've taken care of business."

Her face lit up and she hugged him tightly. The elation she felt at hearing him say that was almost more than she could stand. "That's definitely the best thing I've ever heard of," she said.

His swollen heart pounded with a life it had been missing. "Hey, Butter Fingers," he said, pulling away from her hug. "I'll buy you another coffee if ya promise to hang on to it," he said.

She smiled, charmed. "Shane . . . you are a curious man."

About the author

Renée Angers was born in Scarborough, Ontario, Canada, a small town outside Toronto. After relocating as many times as there are years in her life, she finds a comfortable permanent home in her writing. Her stories and characters, although fictional, are inspired from the many interesting and provocative personalities she has run into during her second career as a musician.

Since expanding her creativity into writing, Angers has worked for several information sources and magazines such as local entertainment periodicals, Upfront, The Crow, and Front Magazine, as well as being the founder and Editor in Chief of the controversial literary e-zine, New Graffiti.

Renée Angers is the author of several published books and is currently working on a screenplay/project with a local filmmaker.

Further information on these titles is available from Renée Anger's website: www.geocities.com/renkma/

More great titles can be found at www.bladudbooks.com